## This woman...

Her hair, the scent of her skin was all too familiar. He looked at her flushed face and eyes that refused to meet his. He was close enough to feel her presence, to react to her nearness. He was instantly aroused. And that could mean only one thing. He took a moment to tamp down the blood rapidly heating his veins. His senses on overload, his mind spinning, the wildest notion entered his head.

"Gracie?"

"I've got to go. I'm late...for an appointment."

Before he could stop her, she was gone. Memories flashed in his mind. The masquerade ball. Those scents, her aura. He wouldn't have ever guessed. But he'd never reacted to a woman like that before.

He stood. Blinking his eyes, he knew only one thing. He had to get to the bottom of this.

He had to *know* for sure.

Was it her?

\* \* \*

*One Night in Texas* by Charlene Sands is part of the Texas Cattleman's Club: Rags to Riches series.

Dear Reader,

Hello and welcome to the final story in the Rags to Riches series of the Texas Cattleman's Club! My story revolves around beautiful lottery winner Gracie Diaz and the deadly handsome, ambitious business tycoon Sebastian Wingate (think Justin Hartley). Gracie's family once worked for the Wingates, but her recent reversal of fortune gives us a story rich with hidden secrets, betrayals and steamy romance.

Sebastian has always been a winner. He's used to having his way in the world. But when Gracie's secrets are revealed to him, Sebastian fights tooth and nail to know the woman who has haunted his dreams. And Gracie isn't ready to let her onetime secret crush into her heart, now that their circumstances have changed.

It was truly a pleasure to bring *One Night in Texas* to you. I hope you enjoy revisiting the characters from the Texas Cattleman's Club and find the answers you are looking for in Gracie and Sebastian's story!

As always, happy reading!

*Charlene Sands*

# CHARLENE SANDS

—

# ONE NIGHT IN TEXAS

Special thanks and acknowledgment are given
to Charlene Sands for her contribution to the
Texas Cattleman's Club: Rags to Riches miniseries.

Recycling programs
for this product may
not exist in your area.

ISBN-13: 978-1-335-23265-6

One Night in Texas

Copyright © 2021 by Harlequin Books S.A.

This edition published by arrangement with Harlequin Books S.A.

For questions and comments about the quality of this book,
please contact us at CustomerService@Harlequin.com.

Harlequin Enterprises ULC
22 Adelaide St. West, 40th Floor
Toronto, Ontario M5H 4E3, Canada
www.Harlequin.com

Printed in U.S.A.

Charlene Sands is a *USA TODAY* bestselling author of contemporary romance and stories set in the American West. She's been honored with the National Readers' Choice Award, the CataRomance Reviewers' Choice Award and is a double recipient of the Booksellers' Best Award. Her 2014 Harlequin Desire was named the Best Desire of the Year.

Charlene knows a little something about romance—she married her high school sweetheart! And her perfect day includes reading, drinking mocha cappuccinos, watching Hallmark movies and riding bikes with her hubby. She has two adult children and four sweet young princesses who make her smile every day. Visit her at www.charlenesands.com to keep up with her new releases and fun contests. Find her on Facebook, Instagram and Twitter, too: Facebook.com/charlenesandsbooks and Twitter.com/charlenesands.

## Books by Charlene Sands

### Harlequin Desire

### *The Slades of Sunset Ranch*

*Sunset Surrender*
*Sunset Seduction*
*The Secret Heir of Sunset Ranch*
*Redeeming the CEO Cowboy*

### *Texas Cattleman's Club: Rags to Riches*

*One Night in Texas*

Visit her Author Profile page at Harlequin.com, or charlenesands.com, for more titles.

You can also find Charlene Sands on Facebook, along with other Harlequin Desire authors, at Facebook.com/harlequindesireauthors.

To my author pal and assistant, Dani Gorman.
You are the best. Thanks for all you do!

# One

She looked at herself in the mirror and saw the same girl she'd always seen staring back at her. Gracie Diaz of Mexican American descent, whose immigrant father had worked for the Wingate family on their ranch, whose mother had taken up waitressing once Gracie's father died. She saw the same young girl with smoky brown eyes, olive skin and long dark hair who was still swept up in romantic fantasies of Sebastian, the more serious of the devastatingly handsome Wingate twins. The same starry-eyed dreamer with lofty aspirations of developing an events business and having a family of her own one day.

But she wasn't *just* that girl anymore… She was much more. Twenty-eight years old now, and the winner of a sixty-million-dollar lottery—a woman with means to do as she pleased.

"And you did that, Gracie," she said to her reflection. "You did as you pleased."

At the Texas Cattleman's Club masquerade ball. Nearly three months ago, she'd fallen for a tall, masked stranger, unable to resist his enigmatic charm. There was something in the way he'd held her, danced with her, *kissed* her. He was masterful and passionate, and it all had been so thrilling. She'd tossed away her inhibitions that night and had given in to the cravings of the body and mind. His scent, his deep, low voice, the way he moved—their chemistry had been off the charts. Their secret tryst had happened quickly, in a hidden spot where they wouldn't be found. But mere moments after they'd made love, voices coming from the hallway had interrupted their erotic interlude, and she'd fled. Taken off without so much as getting his name.

The mystery had intrigued her for months.

Because Gracie didn't know who he was.

*Until now.*

Her cell phone rang and she picked up on the second ring. Smiling into the phone, she said, "Hi, Beth."

She'd been Beth Wingate's assistant before she'd won the lottery, and now they worked side by side on special events. But mostly, Beth was her dearest friend. She hadn't told her friend the truth yet because she hadn't had enough time to process what she'd discovered two weeks ago. But she knew she couldn't keep it under wraps forever. "I'm glad you called me back."

"I know why you're worried, hon," Beth replied. "But believe me, you buying the Wingate Estate isn't gonna put my nose out of joint. I'm actually *glad* you're doing it, Gracie, because ultimately, it's good for everyone. My family needs cash to get Wingate Enterprises up to par. And selling the estate is the best way to get the new Wingate hotel chain on its feet."

Gracie was grateful to Beth for her encouragement. Though she had always dreamed of living in this amazing estate, she'd never believed it would happen. She'd chalked it up to one silly girl's childhood fantasy. After all, she'd been the daughter of a ranch employee, her father working for the Wingates most of his life. So now it was a pretty strange feeling having this monetary reversal, to be in the position to buy the estate. She'd never thought herself worthy and maybe she didn't feel that way now, either. But her mentor's supportive words had helped. "Thanks for making me feel better about it, Beth."

But it wasn't just the Wingate heiress's opinion that mattered. Soon Gracie would have to deal with Beth's brother Sebastian. She *so* wasn't looking forward to that.

"It's the truth," Beth said. "I'm happy you and the baby will be living there. How are you feeling lately?"

"My morning sickness is gone, thank the Lord for that. And I feel pretty good. No baby bump yet, but the doctor says I'm healthy."

"All good news. You've been wanting a family of your own for a long time now. It's finally happening."

Gracie closed her eyes, filled with mixed emotions. After she'd won the lottery, she'd tried dating, but she was never sure if it was her or her money that attracted men to her. After several dating mishaps, her trust had evaporated and she'd pretty much decided to have a baby on her own. She'd seen Dr. Everett months ago for fertility treatment, planning to do in vitro, but a glorious one-night stand during the masquerade ball had taken care of that. Now she was three months pregnant by a man she'd crushed on during her youth, a man who'd never seemed interested in her in the least, a man whose identity she'd finally figured out. "Yes, it finally is."

She placed her hand over her belly, imagining the new life growing inside her. What a miracle it was. She'd wanted a family of her own so much, and now those cherished dreams were *finally* coming true. She loved this baby already, but she didn't love the strings that would eventually become attached.

She'd have to think about that tomorrow.

Today, she had an estate to purchase.

"Beth, I'm glad we spoke. You've been such a good friend, and I didn't want to do anything that would make it awkward between us."

"Nothing ever will, girlfriend."

"Same here. Well, gotta run. I'll call you in a few days, okay?"

"Sounds good. Oh, and, Gracie…good luck."

"Thanks."

Gracie set the phone down and chewed on her lip. She was at loose ends here, and needed to gather her wits. After all, she had a meeting at the foreclosed Wingate Estate in one hour.

With her Realtor, her attorney...*and the father of her baby.*

It was damn cold inside the house, the January chill sweeping into the walls of the empty estate. Sebastian shuddered. From the frigidness? Or was it from a sudden feeling of loss? All the furnishings inside the house were gone, most items hauled off to an estate company where they'd gotten a fair price, but nowhere near the cost of his family's memories.

Sebastian wasn't the sentimental type—he was a realist and this sale was a good thing—but still, he was hit with a wave of unexpected nostalgia from selling his childhood home. There'd been an abundance of love here, plus silly and not-so-silly arguments. Not to mention wild shenanigans, especially between him and his twin brother, Sutton. His other siblings—Miles, Harley and Beth—hadn't exactly been angels, either. Sebastian grinned, thinking of his brothers and sisters when they were kids. He'd allow himself a moment to reminisce about the good times, the pranks they'd pulled, the trouble the five of them would get into. There was never a dull moment in the Wingate household.

But their good name had almost been taken down by sabotage. All the Wingates had worked toward this past year had nearly been destroyed.

In a big way, their home was the answer to the Wingates' prayers. Once this place was sold, Sebastian would have cold hard cash to put into the relaunch of the Wingate name and reputation, as well as the financial means to invest in a hotel chain geared for romantic getaways, wedding events and resort-style fun.

For years, their hotels throughout the world accommodated the corporate class. They were straightforward residences meant to temporarily house business and industry travelers. Now, with the money from the estate sale, conference rooms would be converted into grand ballrooms, cafeterias would become gourmet dining rooms and cooks would be replaced with culinary chefs. The atmosphere and attitude associated with Wingate would change entirely. It had to work. The Wingate empire was banking on it.

The door opened and in walked Gracie Diaz. Oh, man, she looked *good*—her lustrous dark hair down and parted to the side, and her delectable body rocking a clingy dress. With those big, almond-shaped eyes, she could practically destroy a man with one sultry look. Sebastian inhaled a deep breath, giving his addled brain a mental shake. He'd always been attracted to the olive-skinned beauty, but he'd never gotten close. Never acted upon his urges with her, because Gracie had always been off-limits. She was the daughter of an employee. *And* his sister Beth's best friend. Succumbing to his desires spelled disaster at every turn, and Sebastian was smarter than that. But if things were different, he'd be knocking on her door until she let him in.

As soon as Gracie spotted him, she stopped in her

tracks. She seemed really shaken, her usual confidence apparently hitting a bump. He understood why.

She was the one with power now. With money enough to buy their family home, and she wasn't comfortable with it. It was, in a sense, a complete reversal of fortunes.

Sure, the sale was awkward, but completely necessary...and welcome.

"Come in, Gracie. I don't bite."

He smiled, but that only made her mouth turn down.

He walked toward her, taking tentative steps. "Whatever you're thinking, don't," he said. "I can assure you, no one is upset about you buying the estate."

"I understand," she replied tentatively. "Beth told me the same thing."

"Okay, then. Come in. There's a table and chairs set up in the dining room. Your attorney thought it best for us to go over any concerns you have here, so we can address them as they come up."

She stepped inside, skirting around him. "I have no concerns."

"Just in case." And maybe *he* did. As CEO of Wingate Enterprises, he wanted to oversee the sale, to protect his family interests, as well. Old habits died hard.

Gracie took a seat at the table, setting her briefcase on the chair beside her. She'd become quite a businesswoman, from what Beth had told him. Not only had she helped his sister with planning galas and events, but she'd also funded a new eatery in town. She was looking for other investments, too, he'd learned.

But she sure seemed jumpy around him today. Maybe it was the sale of the estate, or maybe it was her pregnancy. Though, by looking at her in a body-hugging soft gray sweater dress that exposed her perfect shape and brought out the lovely tones on her olive skin, she didn't look pregnant at all. No, she looked gorgeous and *hot*.

His mind wandered to a place it shouldn't go. A place he tried to never let it go. He'd become pretty darn good at pushing aside his attraction for Gracie Diaz.

Luckily, he didn't have to think on it too hard, because the attorneys and Gracie's Realtor, Tom Riley, walked in just then, and within a minute, they'd made introductions and gotten right down to business.

The negotiations went smoothly, if you could call them that. Gracie had asked for nothing out of the ordinary. And they'd agreed to all the terms laid out by both attorneys. Gracie had even agreed to rehire some of the staff and groundskeepers for the property. She was a woman who understood hard work and didn't take anything for granted. After her father passed, she'd started waitressing to put herself through online college. Sebastian admired that trait. He was a hard worker, too, sometimes to a fault. At times, his staff would remind him of the late hour, and his twin would tell him to take a damn vacation. Sutton never kept his thoughts to himself, especially around his older brother by three minutes, but Sebastian wasn't one to listen.

"So if both sides are happy, I'll draw up the necessary papers," Tom Riley said. He gave Gracie an encouraging nod, as if to say all was in order and the deal would be done soon.

She smiled softly. Which had Sebastian oddly on edge. He should be satisfied—after all, it was what Wingate Enterprises needed, a financial boost in the arm. Yet, he couldn't take his eyes off Gracie. She'd barely said a word throughout the talks, and her smile just now was the first one she'd cracked since she'd gotten here. Instead, she'd tapped her fingers on the table, toyed with the hem of her sweater dress—something he'd *tried* not to notice.

But those long tan legs weren't easy to ignore.

He'd known Gracie for years. She was a family friend and they'd always been civil with each other, despite his hidden fascination to her, yet he'd never seen her looking so nervous.

"I think we have a real workable deal," he said to her Realtor.

His attorney, Todd Woodbury, seemed pleased. "I think everything's in order." He began to gather the papers, stuffing them into his briefcase.

"Well, then, I guess we're good to go." Sebastian smiled at Gracie, but she didn't make eye contact. What was with her? Why wouldn't she give him the time of day?

"I'll show you out," he told the men. Not that he had a right to usher them out; he didn't own the house any longer. And hadn't lived here for months. He was living in a rental house now, but he had to make sure

Gracie was okay with this. "I want a minute to speak to Ms. Diaz alone."

He walked them out and turned to find Gracie, who was snatching up her briefcase and a pile of papers. She then made a mad dash for the door, but halfway there she fumbled, and the papers went flying, practically landing at his feet. He bent to retrieve them. "I'll get these."

"No, it's okay," she said, dropping down on her knees to gather them up. Their heads nearly bumped as both grabbed for the papers, and that was when he caught a whiff of her hair as it fell forward in long, glimmering straight sheets. He breathed deeper, taking it in. That floral scent reminded him of something...

And then a hint of her perfume reached his nostrils. It was wildly erotic. The mysterious scents that had haunted him for weeks were all here.

He hadn't stopped thinking of that woman, of their one-night stand, which had been crazy and amazing and *intoxicating*. He'd lain awake nights wondering who she was, and why he couldn't figure it out. Wondering if he would ever find her.

And wondering if he'd ever have better sex. He'd relived that night in his mind so many times, recalling how creamy smooth her skin was, how delicious her lips tasted, how silky her hair was. All of it came rushing back now. The scent of her hair, the texture of her skin, the soft moans as she came apart in his arms...

In his gut, he knew he'd found his mystery woman. And it was none other than Gracie Diaz.

He looked at her flushed face and downcast eyes, which blatantly refused to meet his. He was close enough to feel her presence, to react to her nearness. Like some damn high school boy with raging hormones, he was instantly aroused. And that could only mean one thing. He took a moment to tamp down the blood rapidly heating his veins. His senses on overload, his mind began to spin.

"Gracie?"

She stole the papers from his hands and rose quickly. "I've really got to go. I'm late…for an appointment."

Before Sebastian could stop her she was gone, leaving him kneeling there as she sprinted out the door. More memories flashed in his mind of the masquerade ball. Those erotic scents, the sensual aura of her. He wouldn't have ever guessed it. But he'd never reacted to a woman like that before.

He stood up and swallowed down his misgivings. Blinking his eyes, he knew only one thing. He had to get to the bottom of this. He had to *know* for sure.

And the only way to do that was to confront her.

Gracie paced the floor in her living room, wringing her hands, feeling anything but hungry. But it was dinnertime now and she had to eat, for the baby's sake. So she'd called for takeout, something she could stomach, and the pizza delivery guy was due here any minute.

At least she'd ordered a healthy veggie pizza with all her favorite toppings. Maybe her appetite would come back. Right now she was bordering on nausea. Not from her pregnancy, no, she'd been pretty healthy lately on that score. But from the fact that she was fairly sure Sebastian had put two and two together today, and figured out she was the woman behind the mask, the woman he'd made love to with unequaled passion.

What else had he figured out? It wasn't exactly rocket science. They'd been together three months ago, and she was three months pregnant.

Her heart skipped a beat every time she thought about him being her mysterious lover. She'd found out quite by accident during a party just weeks ago, when Sebastian had been tossed into a pool and she'd seen the scar on his back, the one she remembered feeling while they were making wild, passionate love that night. She'd been shocked to her very core, totally blown away to learn that Sebastian, her teenage crush, was the guy who'd fathered her child.

Sebastian had never thought of her as anything but a family friend. He'd never given her a second look. In the back of her mind, she'd always thought it was because she wasn't worthy. There was a definite class difference between them. Even if the Wingates didn't make it obvious, Gracie had always *felt* it. She wasn't good enough for a Wingate, and she'd never once thought her fantasies of Sebastian would ever come true.

The knock at her door made her jump. Gosh, she was a nervous Nelly today. She grabbed her credit card and strode to the door, her appetite at an all-time low. But she thought of the baby's health and gently opened the door.

"Pizza delivery." It was Sebastian, holding the square box.

Her eyes widened. *What on earth?* Then she heard the rumble of an engine, and saw the delivery guy take off in his tiny blue car.

"You can put your credit card away, I paid for it."

"I…don't understand. Why are you here?"

"For pizza?"

She shook her head.

"Okay, I think you know why. We need to talk."

"Showing up unannounced isn't polite."

"Neither is lying," he said brusquely. "Are you going to let me in?"

She paused. She had no choice. "I suppose I have to. You have my dinner." Not that she could eat a bite now.

She moved aside and let him into the foyer of her small, tastefully decorated rental home. His presence filled the space, surrounding her, making her nerves bounce. They stared at each other for a split second, then Gracie grabbed the box. He didn't let it go. Four hands on one pizza box. "I've got it," he said. "Where's the kitchen?"

Her shoulders slumped as she released the box, pivoted and led the way into the kitchen. The instant gleam of white cabinets and sparkling countertops contrasted with her gloomy mood. She was totally unprepared for this sudden visit. Because, in truth, she was still processing this baby-daddy bombshell, and hadn't thought far enough into the future to know what to say to Sebastian if ever confronted. But here he was, his eyes probing, his very kissable mouth looking thin and hard.

He slid the box onto the table and put his hands on his hips, as if he were the ruler of the kingdom or something. A ruler dressed in black slacks, a white shirt rolled up at the sleeves and tight enough across his broad chest to leave any sane woman breathless. Aside from the way his presence unnerved her, she wasn't going to let him get the best of her.

"You're her, the woman from the masquerade ball, aren't you?"

"I was at the ball, yes." She turned away from him and opened the pizza box. The scent of bell peppers, olives and tomatoes wafting up curled her stomach. She closed the box.

"Don't dance around the subject, Gracie. Look at me."

Gracie didn't like to be ordered around. She didn't like that he'd trapped her. Especially since she hadn't sorted this all out in her mind yet. When she didn't turn around, he walked over to face her fully, his presence looming. He was in her space, inches away, probing her with eyes that demanded an answer, with his tight, firm mouth. It was hard to imagine that mouth on hers, like it had been months ago. It was hard to believe she'd given him so much that night and now he was here interrogating her.

"I already told you I was at the ball." She lifted her chin.

"It's the reason you've been so skittish around me today."

"I'd just spent a fortune on your house. So yes, I was anxious."

"Gracie, dammit. Answer my question."

She had nowhere to go. No way to put him off any longer. She didn't want to admit this to herself, much less to him. But she hesitated too long.

Sebastian put a finger to her cheek and his soft touch melted her instantly. She hated that he could do that to her, crumble her defenses that way. "Gracie, it was you, wasn't it?"

She swallowed and gave a nod.

Breath blew out of his mouth and he stepped back, looking differently at her now. As if he was reliving that night in his mind, thinking of the sexy, erotic things they'd done to each other. He seemed truly shocked. As if he couldn't believe *she* could cause that reaction in him. Her pride could barely take the insult.

"When did you know?" he asked gruffly.

"What does it matter?"

*"When?"*

"I found out at the launch party. I saw…the scar on your back when you got out of the pool. I remembered it." That night, in their secret alcove, there was no light, only heat and passion, and their heightened senses. She'd remembered tracing her fingertips over that scar, recalled wondering how he'd gotten it.

For a second, Sebastian looked away, as if touching upon the moment he and his brother Sutton had been celebrating the launch of their new hotel. One second he'd been standing by the pool, and the next he'd been tossed in. It had all been fun and games, until Gracie saw him strip off his wet shirt and get naked from the waist up, and that was when she'd noticed the scar.

Sebastian turned and stared into her eyes. "I've never forgotten that night, Gracie."

Neither had she. It was the night she'd had incredible sex. The night she'd conceived her baby. "Getting tossed into the pool?"

"I'm not talking about that night, and you know it. I'm talking about the masquerade ball."

"Oh, right." Playing dumb wasn't her strong suit. She was stalling.

"And the baby you're carrying…it's mine?"

She set her hand over her belly. It was *hers*. All hers. Sebastian wasn't her fantasy man any longer. She didn't want a man who didn't want her and he'd proven that to her over the years. He'd never given her a second look before. He'd never flirted or seemed the least bit interested in her; and now to think Sebastian was the man who'd made wild love to her was all so confusing. His questioning rattled her brain. She wasn't ready to sort through her muddled thoughts—she needed more time. "The baby is mine. We want nothing from you."

"What?"

"Sebastian, that night we were two strangers meeting. It wasn't planned. And so you owe us nothing."

"Hey, listen to me, Gracie. Maybe that night was a

mistake, but I don't run out on my mistakes and obligations. And you have no right—"

"This…baby…is…not…a mistake." Heat rose up her neck. Her face felt flush. "It's wanted. By me."

"I didn't say the baby was a mistake, Gracie. It's just that you need to think about this more rationally."

"You think I'm not being rational? I'm being very rational. I want what's best for my baby."

"*Our* baby."

Gracie sucked in a big breath. She felt faint. Probably because she hadn't eaten all day. So what she needed now more than anything was to show Sebastian the door.

"Why don't we sit down and discuss this?" he asked.

"No, I'm tired. I think you should go."

"Gracie?"

"Sebastian, just go. I need to rest." She was playing the pregnancy card, but it was true. The day had taken a toll on her.

"We haven't finished this. Hell, we haven't even started it. I'll call you tomorrow."

She nodded and marched to her front door, leaving him to follow. All she wanted right now was to get him out of her house. She needed some peace.

At the entrance, Sebastian faced her, his expression somewhere between panic and remorse. Already he'd insulted her, said she was irrational and called the baby she was carrying a mistake. "Gracie, I, uh… I'll call you," he repeated.

"Fine." It was so *not* fine. But she wanted him to go,

and if agreeing to talk to him tomorrow would do the trick, then so be it.

"Get some sleep." He gave her a sweeping look that touched every nerve in her body. Then he walked out.

# Two

Gracie spent the morning in her pajamas, looking on-line for baby furniture. Sipping decaf coffee and eating a blueberry scone on her bed was a good way to distract herself from the confrontation she'd had with Sebastian last night. She fully expected him to call her first thing this morning, but it was already eleven o'clock and the phone hadn't rung once.

She clicked on page after page of cribs and dressers, of high chairs and strollers and all things baby. It was clearly daunting. She'd always wanted a child, but now with all these choices in front of her, she definitely had homework to do. At some point she would take a class on parenting and childbirth. Gosh, her tummy rumbled in excitement and a little fear.

Though Sebastian Wingate had played a role in her fantasies from childhood, it was a mere silly young girl's dream. Gracie wanted the kind of unconditional love her parents had had for each other. It was clear Sebastian didn't have feelings for her.

And the fact was, she really didn't know him at all. Was he the man of her childhood fantasies or the mystery man who'd swept her off her feet and made love to her? How often had she thought about that one wondrous night with Sebastian, and the wild woman she'd become in his arms? It had been so out of character for her, to have sex with a stranger. But the pull between them had been strong. Undeniable. *Uncontrollable*. He'd given her an unforgettable night of mind-blowing passion.

And a baby.

She had to think about what that all meant.

She was still processing it when her cell phone rang, jerking her out of her musings.

Her stomach ached. This was the call she'd prayed wouldn't happen, but as she dared a look on the phone screen, Lauren's face popped up. The breath trapped in her throat slowly escaped and her shoulders slumped in relief. Lauren Roberts was her friend, and now they were business partners anticipating the grand opening of The Eatery in just one week. The restaurant was almost ready, the staff hired. Lauren was an amazing chef, someone who'd started a food truck business that kept her hopping. Now she was selling those trucks to commit to one place, and one man. Sutton Wingate,

Sebastian's identical twin brother. The couple were head over heels in love and planning a wedding, but she wouldn't hold that against her friend. Sutton was actually a pretty cool guy.

"Hi, Lauren. I was planning on meeting you in a few hours at The Eatery. What's up?"

"Uh, that's why I'm calling. Something's…come up, and I was hoping you could come by maybe a little earlier?" Her voice squeaked. "I'll make your favorite lunch. The baby will like it, too, I promise."

Lauren seemed unusually anxious. "I have no doubt. You wouldn't have it any other way. Let's see, I could be there by noon. Does that work?"

"Yes, thanks. That'll be…um, perfect."

"Lauren, is everything okay?"

There was a short pause on the other end of the phone. "Yes… I think so."

"We're still going to go over the plans for the grand opening, right? I have some ideas to run by you."

"Y-yes. We'll do that. Uh, okay, gotta run."

Gracie held the receiver long after the call ended, thinking her friend sure had acted odd over the phone. She'd find out what was going on once she saw Lauren face-to-face.

A few minutes after twelve, Gracie unlocked the back door of The Eatery and let herself in. She passed the small room where Lauren and her sous-chefs would taste-test new items on the menu, then walked into the state-of-the-art kitchen. After the appliances had been installed, she'd teased Lauren that their sparkle and shine could blind a person when they walked in. Even now, she could smell the newness of the place. "Lauren, I'm here," she called out.

Lauren walked in from the main dining room, wearing an apron. "Hi," she said, out of breath.

"Hi."

"I was just serving your lunch at your favorite table."

"You mean *our* lunch, don't you?"

Lauren's face colored to a rosy pink and she reached for both of her hands and gave a squeeze. "Gracie, we're good friends now, aren't we? And you know I value this partnership very much, right?"

Where was all this coming from? Lauren seemed super serious and it worried her. Gracie nodded. "Of course."

"Good, because I really care about you."

"I care about you, too."

She heard someone walking into the main dining room and glanced out the kitchen doorway. "I didn't know Sutton was meeting us for lunch, too."

Lauren closed her eyes briefly. "That's not Sutton."

Gracie dropped her friend's hands. "What?"

"It's Sebastian."

"I don't want to talk to him right now," she whispered in a rush. She wasn't ready; that was why she'd sent him away last night. The last thing she wanted to do was speak to him face-to-face. Seeing him in the flesh confused her even more. Because he was undeniably handsome, and when she looked at him, memories flashed in her mind. Of him kissing her, caressing her, making love to her like she was the only woman on earth. It had been so good between them—being totally in tune with her body, Sebastian had given her the best night of her life. But she feared him, too, because he could interfere with her plans for the baby. He could change everything. And that worried her.

Before she could utter another word, Sebastian walked into the kitchen. "Don't blame Lauren. She didn't want to do this. Honestly, it took all my powers of persuasion and then some to convince her to help me."

She glanced from Sebastian to Lauren. "Did he hold a gun to your head?"

Lauren smiled softly, her eyes filled with compassion. "No, just a baby. Gracie, I'm sorry. Please forgive me."

"So…you know?"

"I do. Sebastian confided in me. And honestly, I think it's pretty amazing."

Gracie blinked. She was trapped by her friend's good intentions. The truth was bound to come out eventually. She and Lauren had discussed their special masquerade ball encounters with each other. Lauren and Sutton had also met under the guise of a mask at the gala, and there'd been a case of mistaken identity between the twin brothers. But they'd fallen in love despite the mix-up, and now were embarking on their happily-everafter. "But, Lauren, you took Sebastian's side over mine. We're supposed to be partners."

"I didn't think of it as taking sides. You both need to

talk and you can do it here. In private. With no interruptions. Will you do that?"

She shrugged, defeated. "Only because I have no choice."

"Okay, sorry. You two have some lunch together. And if you're still speaking to me after that, I'll come back and we can talk shop."

Gracie tipped her chin up toward the ceiling, shaking her head the way her mother would often do when she was faced with a difficult situation. Both coconspirators awaited her response. "Fine."

"Okay, well, I'll disappear now." Lauren gave a tentative smile. "Everything is set out and ready for you. I made your favorite, Gracie."

"Thank you," she said quietly. It was a really sweet gesture, one that might just let Lauren off the hook.

Gracie tried to ignore the earnest look on Sebastian's face—the small smile, not of triumph, if she was being honest, but of optimism. He strode by her side, almost making an attempt to put his hand to her back, but then corrected the move. Smart man. She wasn't in the mood to be charmed.

At the table, he pulled out the chair for her and she took her seat. Around her, unique Southwestern artwork decorated the top half of the walls, while ocean-blue glass tiles added color and light and sparkle to the lower half. Fresh and clean, a place for open minds and palates, The Eatery encapsulated Lauren's vibrant personality to the letter.

"Looks delicious," Sebastian said, glancing at the

lobster roll bathed in a reduction of lemongrass sauce and paired with skinny fries and zucchini spirals.

"It is. Lauren's creations got me hooked and I wanted to help her. When I worked with Beth, I'd leave the Wingate Estate at night and head over to one of Lauren's trucks. Those meals were my go-to and I was never disappointed. I'm excited for her, for this place."

"Yeah…about Lauren," Sebastian murmured, taking a breath. "She's a friend of mine, too, and I put undue pressure on her to make this lunch happen."

"You have a rep for getting what you want."

He let that comment slide. "So it won't hurt your relationship with her?"

"I'm not happy, but her intentions were good."

"I'm glad you recognize that."

"Yeah, well, at least it's one thing I recognized." She stared straight into his eyes. How could she not know she was making love with Sebastian, when she'd dreamed of it so many times?

"You could say that about me, too," he said. "Listen, I think we got off to a bad start yesterday. Can I have a mulligan?"

"Golf terms are so not persuasive."

"Sorry. How about giving me a second chance?"

"I don't have much choice, now, do I?"

"Maybe we should break bread together. That would be a start. Are you hungry? Or did you lose your appetite when you saw me?"

She laughed. Though she hated to, because yesterday he'd called the baby a mistake. But he had charm.

What woman would look at him and lose her appetite? "I need to eat."

"Yes, you do."

They sat quietly and chowed down, and every once in a while, their eyes would meet. Sebastian had the most unique green eyes. She'd memorized the change of colors, in her head. Sometimes they were soft and pale like a shallow river, and sometimes they were probing and deep like a lush forest, depending on his mood or the color he wore.

Today he was dressed in casual, well-worn jeans and a white shirt, looking terribly handsome and manly. An unwelcome thrill scurried through her body while sitting with him, sharing a meal. They'd done far more than this as two disguised strangers, getting naked and making love in secret, giving to each other unselfishly. She's never been that bold before, and her masked lover had encouraged her with his whispered words, his guttural groans. That, too, had been thrilling, but *this*? This was surreal. Ever since finding out that Sebastian was the father of her child, she'd been overwhelmed and riddled with confusion and deep emotion. And now she was dining with him, just like she'd often daydreamed.

She nibbled on her sandwich and picked at her baked skinny fries. Sebastian had already finished his food and was watching her. "Just to clarify," she said, pointing a fry at him, "this baby is *not* a mistake."

"I was the one who made the mistake, Gracie. I didn't mean what I said yesterday."

"Good."

"So you accept my apology?"

"I haven't heard an apology."

He reached across the table and covered her hand, looked straight into her eyes. "I'm sorry, Gracie. I truly am."

The instant he touched her, her pulse pounded and an electric jolt shot through her. He squeezed a little harder, closing his eyes as if…he couldn't help himself. As if he felt the connection, too. He muttered an oath and she couldn't blame him. They seemed to share something combustible. So it hadn't been just the excitement of the masquerade, or the thrill of a clandestine tryst. Their attraction was as real now as it'd been that night. Gracie tugged her hand away, conceding that one touch from him was all that was needed to unravel her.

Sebastian stared into her eyes. "Do you forgive me?"

Oh, gosh. She didn't want to. But her mama had taught her to forgive if the asker was sincere, and Sebastian's deep green eyes spoke of sincerity times a thousand. Which meant she would have to give him the benefit of the doubt. "Yes."

"I want to be a part of your life, Gracie. Part of the baby's life. He's my…"

"Don't you dare say she's your responsibility."

*"She?"*

"He or she. I won't find out for a while."

"I hope I'm there when you do."

Gracie didn't have a crystal ball and had no clue what the future would bring. After all, when she'd set out on a path to be a businesswoman and a mom, she hadn't figured on dealing with the baby's father. She was supposed to conceive this child by a medical procedure. But clearly, fate had other plans in store for her. "I can't make any promises."

His brows rose, and the softness in those green eyes vanished. "I'm not asking for promises." His lips tightened, all color draining out of them as he gave his head a shake. "Well, hell…yes, I am. You seem to want to do this all on your own. Why is that? Is it because our roles have reversed, and you have the means to raise this baby all by yourself? Tell me, Gracie. Is that it? The Wingates are down right now and you're a millionaire and so it's okay to cut me out of my baby's life?"

The chair slammed back as Gracie instantly rose from her seat. "How dare you accuse me of that!"

Sebastian lifted up, too, gritting his teeth. "Is it true? Are you too damn independent and stubborn to realize that the child deserves two parents in its life? Even if one of them is broke."

Fierce anger bubbled up and she let her hot Hispanic temper fly. "You have no clue about me, Sebastian. You never did." And maybe that was the problem. All those years she'd spent looking up to him, admiring him, measuring all men against him, even when he'd never given her a second glance. Oh, what a fool she'd been. She was the help, or rather the child of the help, and she'd always felt she wasn't good enough to be included in his inner circle. But to accuse her of that very thing was wrong on all kinds of levels. In her heart, she was still the same girl, minus the money, of course, that she'd always been. A girl who deserved to be loved for who she was inside and not for any other reason. "This conversation is over. I'm leaving. Don't even try to follow."

"Wouldn't dream of it."

"Fine."

*"Fine."*

Gracie marched out the back way, and right before she slammed the door, she heard Sebastian mutter, "Ah, crap."

That was exactly how she felt right now.

As well as remorseful and angry and ten other emotions she didn't care to name.

Is it okay for me to return? Lauren sent the text to both him and Gracie. Apparently, his brother's fiancée was an optimist. She'd believed one sit-down would do the trick. And had been thoughtful enough to give them privacy to talk, arrange a delicious lunch for them and set the atmosphere. However, Sebastian had blown it, but only because Gracie had been unreasonable. She wouldn't give an inch.

He'd texted Lauren to come back anytime. They were through.

*Literally.*

Ten minutes later, Lauren entered The Eatery through the back door. "I'm back," she called as she walked into the kitchen. She faced him at the stainless steel sink. "What are you doing?" She looked at the dish towel in his hand.

"I'm cleaning up. It's the least I can do. I messed up your meeting with Gracie."

"I heard."

"Already?"

"Gracie and I had a brief conversation. She's not happy with you." She eyed the dish towel again. "Give me that." He handed it over. "For heaven's sake, you don't need to clean up."

"I wanted to do...something."

"Well, talk to me. Gracie didn't go into detail, but she said you and she—"

"She rattles me, Lauren. I mean, I look at her now, and I see the woman I can't stop thinking about. That night we spent together was..." He wasn't a kiss-and-tell kind of guy. "Let's just say I've never had such a hot night, never felt such an instant connection with a woman." He wanted *that* Gracie, the one who wasn't so damn proud and stubborn. The one who'd given him the best night of his life but whom he couldn't go after, because he'd labeled her off-limits. And now he didn't give a damn about that. He wanted her...and the baby.

"Was it because you didn't know who she was?"

"I won't say that didn't play into it. But there's more to it than that. I mean, it was crazy good between us, like two live wires touching. And afterward, I racked my brain trying to figure out who she was, but I never came up with an answer."

"And Gracie never came to mind?"

He shook his head. "If I'm being honest, no. I've always been attracted to her, but for years I pushed those thoughts out of my head. She wasn't ever an option. She was Beth's employee and a good friend for one, and her father worked for us. So I put her completely out of my head. And then at the meeting yesterday, she dropped some papers and we both bent down to get them. The scent of her perfume, the smell of her hair, the closeness we shared, clued me in."

"Wow."

"Yeah, *wow*."

"I heard it had been pretty amazing between you two," Lauren said. "Gracie didn't go into detail when we spoke of it in the past, but by the way her eyes would glow and her voice would become breathless, it was special for her."

She touched his hand. "What did you say to get her so upset?"

Sebastian sighed. "I got angry and hinted that she had no use for me because my family has been dragged through the mud."

"Hinted?"

"Okay, I accused her of it, but only because I was frustrated. She wasn't giving an inch, and well, I'm not used to being at loose ends like this. I'm glad our name has been cleared, but it's unnerving trying to hold on to Wingate Enterprises. It's been a struggle, but we've managed to retain most of our US holdings, and then a beautiful masked woman comes into my life, bringing some brightness. And I find out Gracie's the one tying me up in knots, buying the Wingate Estate and carrying my child. It's a lot to handle." Sebastian's gut tightened.

"I'm sorry the meeting didn't go as we'd hoped," Lauren said. "But I'm afraid you're going to have to fix this on your own. I risked my partnership and friendship with Gracie by going behind her back. I can't do it again."

Sebastian squeezed her hand. "Don't think I'm not grateful, Lauren. You went above and beyond. My brother's a lucky man, getting a woman like you."

"Thank you for saying that. So what are you going to do?"

"I'm not sure yet." But one thing was certain, he wasn't through with Gracie Diaz yet. Not by a long shot.

"Mom, thanks for coming over," Sebastian said, looking at his mother, who was dressed impeccably in a pastel plaid blazer and beige palazzo pants of the finest material. Her hair was up in her usual fancy bun. There was not a hair out of place on Ava Wingate, ever.

"Hello, Sebastian. How's my son today?"

He smiled and kissed her cheek. "I'm fine, Mom."

He led her into the great room of his rented house, and they both took a seat on the couch. His mother was usually a dynamo, someone with incredible energy and gusto, but he'd noticed her slowing down. She seemed worn out lately, and this past year, learning she'd been deceived by her trusted friend had taken a toll on her. Keith Cooper, who'd been his dad's best friend, had been hopeful of gaining Ava's affection after Sebastian's father died. And when that didn't happen, he'd ended up embezzling funds and nearly destroying Wingate

Enterprises. Luckily, he'd been caught before the entire empire went under, but the fiasco with Keith had taken the wind out of his mother's sails. She'd always been strong, the Wingate rock, a woman who always spoke her mind. But now, she seemed defeated in some ways, taken down a peg. It pained him to see it. "Can I get you anything, Mom? A drink? Something to eat?"

"I'm fine, but it's clear that you're not. I can see it in your eyes, Sebastian. Something's troubling you."

"Actually, I do have news."

"More problems with the company?"

He smiled. "No, Mom. Everything is moving along well with the business. It's not that."

She sat back in her seat. "So then, it's personal?"

"Yes, it's *very* personal. And good news. At least I hope you'll think it's good news. You're going to be a grandmother again."

His sister Harley's son, little Daniel, was four years old. But Ava didn't know him too well. Harley had never really gotten along with their mother. She had left home to raise Daniel overseas and stayed away until just months ago, when she'd come back home and finally told Dr. Grant Everett, Daniel's father, the truth. Now Harley, Grant and Daniel were a family and planning on moving to Thailand.

His mother's mouth dropped open as surprise lit up her eyes. "That's…very good news, I suppose." Then her forehead wrinkled. "I didn't know you were dating someone."

Sebastian scratched his chin. "Yeah, well, about

that… It's a long, involved story and I only just found out myself a couple of days ago. But the bottom line is, Gracie Diaz is pregnant, and the child is mine."

*"Gracie?"* His mother's brows rose. "Why, we've known her for years. You never… I don't think you ever gave her a second glance, Sebastian. Am I wrong about that?"

"No, you're not wrong, Mom. But things change. And well, I'm afraid now things aren't going too well. Every time we try to talk, I get tongue-tied, and it ends up with one of us walking away."

Ava smiled. It was rare to see his mother look so amused.

"It's funny to you?"

"No, not funny. But that's exactly how your father was with me when we first met. He said I made him jittery. And either he'd lose his tongue altogether or say the absolute wrong thing to me."

"Really? I never knew that."

Though his mother always did come off as intimidating, and his dad might've been thrown by her strong personality. But it was probably more their powerful attraction to each other that caused his dad's nerves, just like when Sebastian got near Gracie.

"So what's the plan?" his mother asked.

"I'm not sure. She's pretty set on doing this all on her own."

"You have legal rights, son."

He shook his head. "I'm not willing to go that far. At least not right now. I think she's overwhelmed. And

I don't want to destroy whatever relationship I have with her."

"You have a relationship with her?"

"Not at the moment, but I've got to fix that. She won't answer my calls. Won't respond to my texts."

"Want me to speak with her?"

He studied his mother's serious face. He couldn't ask Ava for help. While well intentioned, she might just make things worse. She wasn't the most tactful person in the world, but he knew she was trying hard to help her family and win them back. "Thanks, Mom, but no. I'll manage. I do have a favor. Only a handful of people know I'm the father, so please keep this a secret. I don't think Gracie needs any more pressure right now. Can I trust you to keep it quiet?"

"Of course."

"I thought you had a right to know," he said.

"Well, you're more thoughtful than Harley was."

"Mom, she was young and very mixed up."

"Yes, I know. What's important now is to keep the entire family together. And that includes the little one you're about to have. Do you know if it's a boy or girl?"

"No, it's too soon for that. When we find out, you'll be the first to know."

"I would appreciate that. Tell me, what do you suppose Gracie wants more than anything?"

"What are you getting at?"

"You want something from her, so give her something that's important to her."

Sebastian paused for a second, deep in thought. She may have something there.

His mother rose from her seat. "I've got an appointment in half an hour. I'm afraid I have to be going."

Sebastian walked over to her. "Thanks for listening, Mom."

"You'll be a good father, Sebastian." She kissed his cheek and took hold of his hand. "I'm confident you'll find a way. You always do." Then she smiled again.

His mother had more confidence in him than he had in himself at times. With Gracie, things were off-balance and that flustered him.

And then a thought struck. His mother's words came back to him. *What do you suppose Gracie wants more than anything?* She'd bought the house on the first day it went on sale. She wanted to live at the estate and raise the baby there. Damn, he did have a little bit of leverage with Gracie.

It was risky. It might backfire and he could end up losing everything. But he wasn't willing to give up on Gracie Diaz just yet. He was drawn to her for so many reasons, and he desperately needed more time with her.

Bottom line? He had to try *something* and this was the best he could come up with.

Gracie had spent the entire week helping Lauren get The Eatery ready for tomorrow's big grand opening. She checked on the menus, made sure the staples, supplies and all the orders were correct. Lauren was a pro, and what Gracie didn't know about food service, her partner made sure to school her in with quick lessons. Gracie did know how to promote, however. She had taken out ads in Royal's newspaper, paid teenagers to distribute flyers in the community and reached out to Lauren's food truck fans to spread the word about The Eatery's grand opening.

There were a few other investments Gracie wanted to look into. For starters, she was set on raising horses, to see her father's dream come true. He'd worked as ranch manager for the Wingate family and often spoke of having his own ranch one day. And it was always her goal to start an event-planning business. After working with Beth on galas and charities, she'd caught the bug. She had a knack for planning, design, decoration and making her vision come to fruition. But today, her focus was all about Lauren and The Eatery.

"It's all so exciting," she said to Lauren. "And a lot of hard work. But I'm sure it'll pay off."

"Exciting and nerve-racking," her friend replied. "This has been a dream of mine for a long time. I only hope I haven't forgotten anything."

"You haven't forgotten a thing. You're a pro and I know it's going to be great. I'll be with you all day tomorrow."

"I appreciate that." Lauren smiled. "You and Sutton have given me so much support."

"You deserve it. You've worked hard for this."

"Thanks."

"Now I think we should lock up and go home and get some rest," Gracie said.

"It's only six."

"And knowing you, your day will start at six in the morning."

"You're right. Let's go." Lauren wrapped her arms around Gracie's shoulders and hugged tight. "The three of us need our rest."

The reference to the baby immediately turned her thoughts to the baby's father. Sebastian was making her crazy, saying the wrong things, and his last accusation had really rattled her. She'd always seen him as a kind, thoughtful, hardworking member of the Wingate family. Where was the man she'd crushed on for years? Was he gone now, taken over by someone she didn't recognize or trust?

Later that evening, Gracie hung up the phone from her Realtor in disbelief. Last week she'd gone to his office to sign the necessary papers for the purchase of the Wingate property, hoping for a short escrow period. After all, the house was just sitting there empty. She was anxious to settle in and the Wingates were eager to get their money. Money that they desperately needed to build back their business. But Tom Riley had just told her there was a holdup. Or rather, a holdout. Sebastian was stalling. He'd given her Realtor one excuse after another regarding signing the final papers for the sale of the house. It'd been eight days already. Without his signature, the deal wouldn't go through as planned.

Sebastian had her back up against the wall. He'd called her every day, and every day she'd put him off.

Now he'd fixed it so *she* would have to call *him*. She could go through her attorney to get to the bottom of this, but Sebastian was well versed in business dealings. He knew how to get what he wanted, and she understood he wouldn't cave until she spoke to him.

Gracie squeezed her eyes closed. All the man had to do was touch her and she melted on the spot. It wasn't fair that he had that kind of power over her. She didn't like not being in control...didn't like not knowing which Sebastian she was dealing with. The decisions she would have to make for the future were too important, and she couldn't allow her confusion and, well, yes, her *desire* for him to get in the way.

If that made her a control freak, okay, she'd own it. She had a baby to consider and she'd do everything in her power to protect her child.

So far, Sebastian had called their night together a mistake, making the child she was carrying a mistake, too. He'd accused her of social climbing, thinking so little of her that he thought she would actually push him away because of his recent lack of wealth. And now he was blackmailing her, for lack of a better word, by holding back the sale of the house.

"Not a way to win friends and influence people," she muttered.

If she was a mean girl, she'd teach him a lesson and back out of the deal entirely, to call his bluff. But backing out would mean hurting all the Wingates, and she didn't want to do that. It would also mean denying herself a beautiful place to live. She'd come to love the estate and had spent a lot of time there while growing up. To throw that all away because Sebastian was being obtuse didn't seem right.

Her cell phone rang, breaking into her thoughts. She glanced at the screen and picked up immediately. At least Sebastian did one thing right—he called her. Just like he had for the past week.

"You do know you're jeopardizing the sale of the estate," she said to him.

"Hello to you, too, Gracie."

"Sebastian, I know what you're doing." Her foot began to tap the floor.

"That's good, because I don't have a clue."

"What are you talking about?" she demanded.

"I mean it, Gracie. I *am* jeopardizing the sale of the estate. Because that's how much I want you. If things go sour, I'll be sabotaging the company's success."

"I'm glad you recognize that."

He huffed out a breath. "I've been trying to get your attention all week."

"So blackmailing me was your answer?"

"*Blackmail* is a strong word."

"What would you call it?"

"I'd say it was…a subtle nudge."

"*Subtle?*" She groaned loud enough for him to hear. "You are delusional."

"*Determined* is a better word."

Gracie was tired of this back-and-forth already. He'd found a way to have things on his terms, and she hated that, but in order to move on with her life, she needed to hear him out. "Okay, fine. What do you propose?" Oh, boy, that was such a bad choice of words. "I mean, what do you want?"

"I think we should talk. The sooner, the better."

"Why, are you afraid I'd back out?" she prodded.

"Maybe. Would you?"

"No, not unless you gave me a good reason to," she answered.

"I won't, I can assure you."

Gracie sighed. "And can you assure me you'll sign the documents?"

"Yes, I'm a man of my word."

Maybe he was, but she didn't like his tactics.

"How about we meet tomorrow?" he asked.

"Tomorrow is impossible. It's the grand opening of The Eatery."

"Oh, right. I forgot."

"I can meet you on Monday."

"That's three days away."

"Yes, and…?"

"Okay, fine," he said grudgingly. "I'll come to you. Monday morning."

She closed her eyes. "Monday morning. And I'll meet you at your office."

He paused, clearly not happy, but he kept his tone neutral. "We'll talk Monday, then."

She could only push so far. "Yes, goodbye."

"Good night, Gracie."

His deep, low rasp brought an onslaught of full-body tingles. That voice with its beckoning tone did things to her. The attraction between them was undeniable, like nothing she'd ever felt before. She couldn't quite separate the man blackmailing her from her childhood crush. It gave her a headache and kept her up at night. She'd been avoiding him for that very reason…kept waiting for her head to clear. Only, it wasn't cooperating.

"Sleep well."

"Same to you," she whispered back, before she even realized her mouth was opening. Sebastian was masterful in so many ways, and even though she was angry with him, she couldn't quite get the night of the masquerade ball out of her mind. His touch, his kiss, the way he made love to her. It had been surreal, and something she would never forget.

She had three days before she had to speak to him. She wouldn't dwell.

Tomorrow was all about The Eatery's grand opening, and helping Lauren realize her dream.

# Three

Royal 7 News showed up during the lunch rush to interview Lauren about her transition from her Street Eats food truck business to her very own eating establishment, the news van parked front and center on the street. Gracie didn't have to do much arm-twisting to get them there. Whenever the Wingate name was bandied about, it made news. Most of the press for the past year had been negative, their good name and reputation ruined, but the Wingate family had pulled together, cleared their name, recouped some of their embezzled cash and were now on the road to recovery.

Gracie stood off to the side listening as Lauren continued speaking to Daniella Moon from Royal 7 News. "I was proud of Street Eats, and loved having those food trucks, but opening my own restaurant has always been my dream," she told the reporter.

"Well, judging from the line outside, your restaurant is going to be a huge hit. Royal can use another dining hot spot. And you're engaged to Sutton Wingate. The Wingates were involved in a big scandal not too long ago. Do you have anything to say about that?"

Lauren paused a second, then gave the reporter a big smile. "I never had any doubt that Sutton and his family would clear their name. They were framed and have been vindicated. That's all behind us now."

"Rumor has it you have a silent partner, none other than Gracie Diaz, the recent winner of the sixty-million-dollar Powerball. How much has her support meant to you?"

"I couldn't have done any of this without Gracie's help. She's backed me in every way, believed in me, and I'm very grateful to her."

The reporter walked over to Gracie. "Miss Diaz, looks like you found a good investment in The Eatery. Business seems to be booming."

Gracie didn't love being in the limelight—she'd had enough of that when she'd first won the lottery—but she answered Daniella Moon's questions and then they took off in their news van.

Back in the kitchen now, Lauren wiped her brow. "Thanks for setting that up. I don't think that interview will hurt business," she said with a grin. "Sorry they put you on the spot, Gracie. I know you don't like being in front of cameras."

"For you and The Eatery, I'll endure a camera in my face."

Then Gracie's happy mood soured when she spotted a tall Texan with blond hair and green eyes striding through the back door.

Until she realized it was Sutton. He waved hello to her and walked straight into Lauren's arms. It was nice to see the two of them so happy. Her friend's dreams were all coming true. Good for her.

Cam and Beth stopped by for a late lunch and Gracie seated them at a table near the kitchen. Beth was not only her dear friend and mentor, she was Sebastian's sister. Beth was marrying rancher Cam Guthrie in a matter of weeks and she couldn't be happier for them. Cam was one of the good guys.

"It's great to see you two. I'm really glad you're here, and, Beth, I miss our brainstorming sessions."

Gracie had worked with Beth for years at the estate, helping her plan events, galas and parties, and she'd enjoyed it so much she hoped to open her own events company one day. Back then, it had been a lofty dream, but today it was actually a possibility.

"Yeah, I've heard about those brainstorming sessions," Cam deadpanned. "According to Beth, they'd turned into margarita parties for two." He gave her a wink.

"Giving away our trade secrets, Beth?" Gracie asked.

"Well, it was when we did our best work," she answered.

Beth turned to speak only to Cam. "Gracie gets a drink in her, and then she lets loose."

Gracie chuckled. "With *ideas*, Beth. And I could say the same about you."

"That's why we made such a good team."

"Well, Lauren will be thrilled that you two are here."

"Of course," Beth said. "Lauren is family. Where else would we be?"

"Uh, planning your wedding, maybe. You guys don't have that much more time." Cam had built Beth the home of her dreams, and they were having a private wedding there in two weeks.

"Beth's got it all covered," Cam said, smiling. "Who better to plan a party than my beautiful fiancée?"

"So true," Gracie admitted.

Beth beamed. "I'm all set." Then her brows gathered. "I think."

"Knowing you, everything will be perfect," Gracie reassured her. "But if you need any help, you can always count on me."

"Thanks, and I might take you up on that. We'll talk later."

"Okay."

Beth scanned over the entire restaurant. "I think I love this place already. The artwork is beautiful." Beth had an eye for those things. Gracie had always admired her good taste.

She handed each one of them a menu. "Check out the menu and I'll have a waitress take your order."

"Sounds good. And, Gracie, congrats. The Eatery

is…something. You played a big part in getting this place opened. I know it's going to do well."

Gracie gave Beth a hug. "Thanks for saying that. Means a lot. Now I'd better check on Lauren. She needs to pace herself or she won't make it to dinner."

By eight thirty the dining room was starting to empty out. Gracie's feet ached and she could only imagine how Lauren felt. She took a seat at a corner booth, coaxing Lauren to do the same. Her friend was on an emotional high, but fatigue registered on her face. "You're beat, but in a good way, Lauren."

"You're right. I am beat. But excited, too. There weren't any glitches today, except for running out of cheesecake. I didn't think it'd be so popular. Tomorrow I'll be better prepared."

"No one complained. You gave everyone free dessert. Can't argue with that."

The front door opened and in walked Sutton. "Maybe not entirely over," Gracie said. "Looks like you have to feed this guy again."

Lauren grinned and rose from her seat. She wrapped her arms around her handsome fiancé and then asked him to sit down. That was when Gracie realized it wasn't Sutton this time, it was Sebastian. He'd caught her off guard once again. She didn't like it. She wasn't too happy, either, about the way her stomach flip-flopped every time the man entered the room. Images of their sizzling hot night flashed in her head and she had trouble purging it, trouble forgetting what it felt like being with him that way.

"Thanks for coming, Sebastian," Lauren said.

"I would've been here sooner, but I had meetings most of the day. Congratulations to both of you. I heard your grand opening was a huge success."

"It was more than I could've imagined," Lauren said on a lovely sigh. "Really awesome."

"Yes, it was pretty amazing." Gracie didn't want to burst Lauren's bubble or in any way put a damper on this night by being rude to Sebastian. He had every right to be here, she supposed. But the second he sat down and pierced her with those melt-your-heart green eyes, her pulse pounded and her breath stuck in her throat.

"I bet you haven't eaten, Sebastian. And I know you haven't had a bite to eat since lunch, Gracie. You both need sustenance. Let me get you something wonderful from the kitchen."

"I don't want to put you to work," Sebastian protested. "I'm fine."

"Me, too," Gracie said. "I'll eat later."

"Nonsense. Gracie, you've been a godsend today, and you *need* to eat."

Her point was well taken without the mention of the baby. Although Sebastian's eyes did immediately rivet to her belly. She flushed, her skin prickling under his scrutiny.

"And, Sebastian, I know how you Wingates roll. I bet you're hangry."

He stared straight at Gracie, giving her another unnerving moment. "Okay, I guess I could eat."

"Thanks for not making me argue," Lauren said. "I'll be back in a few minutes."

After Lauren walked off, Sebastian smiled. "She's perfect for my brother."

"I agree."

"Well, that's good. We agree on something. It's a start."

"Sebastian, please let's not talk about anything tonight. I'm really tired."

"You've been here all day?"

She nodded. "It's been fun, seeing a business start off from its very roots. I've never been a part of something like this before."

"You have a mind for business, Gracie."

She shrugged. "Maybe. I have some investment ideas."

"Care to share?"

She shook her head. "Not at the moment. You know, it's uncanny how I almost can't tell you and Sutton apart. He was here today, and when you walked in just now, I thought you were him for a second."

"Yeah, we've gotten that all of our life. You said, *almost*. Does that mean you can tell us apart sometimes?"

Gracie hesitated, biting her lip.

"Well?"

"I, uh…"

"You feel it, too. This pull between us. When I get close, you know it's me."

She closed her eyes briefly. She didn't want to say it aloud. She didn't want him to know.

"I guess I have my answer," he said quietly.

No triumph, no smugness. Just truth.

She nodded. It was the most she was willing to give as admission. Up until now, she hadn't spoken of it, hadn't acknowledged the draw between them. But it was there. It was *real*. She felt it every time he walked into the room. But she still really didn't know Sebastian, the father of her baby. She still didn't know what he wanted from her. Or if she could trust him.

"Gracie," he whispered.

But before he could say anything more, Lauren arrived with a savory chicken-and-rice dish with yeast biscuits and a quinoa salad for them to share.

Sebastian took his eyes off her to glance at the meal. "Looks delicious."

"Yes, uh, thanks." Gracie's stomach growled in a delicate way, but enough to turn their heads. She gasped and put her hands over her tummy. And everyone laughed. "I guess I'd better eat, or this little one is going to be making more noise."

It was the first light moment she'd had with Sebastian, and the brightness in his eyes and on his face was appealing as hell. They smiled at each other, and suddenly, a weight seemed to lift from her shoulders. The boulder that sat there was being chipped away, so she could look at him and see someone she'd known, the boy from her youth, the thoughtful, kind, yet aloof guy she'd had fantasies about. He'd been the quiet one, the more serious of the Wingate twins, and she'd liked that about him.

"Feed that kid, would you?" Lauren teased.

"I plan to."

"And I plan to make sure she eats all of…"

Gracie raised her brows.

Sebastian took one look at her and cut off his own sentence. Was he about to say something to tick her off again? "Nothing, never mind."

"Okay, well, enjoy the meal," Lauren said and walked away again.

After that, Sebastian measured his words carefully and they made it through the meal without a problem.

The kitchen closed by nine thirty and an exhausted Lauren was grateful Sutton stopped by to pick her up. They offered to walk Gracie to her car out back.

Sebastian spoke up instantly. "I'll do it, you two go on home."

"No one needs to walk me," Gracie said. "I'll be just fine."

The look on Sebastian's face said he wasn't going to give in. "I'm going to make sure of it. Put on your jacket and let's go. No arguing, okay?"

Gracie had little choice. She grabbed her jacket and Sebastian helped her put it on.

Lauren locked up The Eatery and then both couples headed in different directions in the parking lot.

Within a few moments, Gracie reached her car. She turned to face Sebastian. "This is it." She drove a sporty cranberry-red Lexus with a small back seat and trunk.

But as much as she loved it, she knew it simply wouldn't suffice once the baby arrived. Buying a family car was on her long list of things to do.

There was a chill in the January air and she shivered a bit.

"Cold?" he asked.

"A little. I'd better get going." She gestured to her car.

"Just one more thing, Gracie."

Sebastian touched her hand just as she was reaching for the door handle. His hand on hers did silly things to her insides. She put her head down, closed her eyes. "What is it?"

"Talk to me, Gracie."

"We'll talk on Monday."

"Gracie," he said softly, as if her name was something precious, something beautiful. "I want to see you before Monday."

She looked up and gazed into his clear green eyes. "Why?"

"You know why."

"But I don't...not really." She had questions. Not quite trusting this.

"Maybe this will help you understand." And then his fist gently lifted her chin, and he bent his head, slowly inching toward her. She couldn't pull away, even if she wanted to. It was crazy, this attraction, this magnetic pull she had toward him. His breath touched her cheek, his lips closed in and the anticipation nearly undid her. She sucked in a breath and he caught that breath with his mouth as his lips careened down onto hers. It was as perfect a kiss as she'd ever had—the perfect taste, the perfect pressure, the perfect sensual mating of their mouths.

His scent surrounded her, his warmth protected her and his arms wrapped around her. She was taken by the power of his kiss. Her body hummed inside and the easy slide of attraction heated her up.

"Sebastian," she whispered, breaking off the kiss. "This isn't a good idea." But it was too late. The kiss marked her, the kiss made her want more. Even as he stopped and pulled away, the damage was done to her soul.

"Gracie, what if you're wrong?"

What if she was wrong? Would she miss out on something wonderful?

Her chest was pounding. If she fell for this guy, it could all go bad quickly. Wasn't it better to keep her distance? Wasn't it better not to give in to this fierce temptation? The fire might burn out and then where would she be? Whenever Sebastian was near, whenever he kissed her, her mind muddied up. She didn't like being confused like this. "What…what do you want from me?"

"A chance to get to know you, Gracie. That's all," he rasped.

"What does that mean?"

Sebastian's smile devastated her. Her heart pounded even harder. "It means I want to date you, Gracie. I want to see where this goes. You owe me."

She blinked. "How do I owe you?"

He sighed deeply, and she sensed his frustration. "You found out it was me at the masquerade ball, and you never said a word. You conceived my child that night, and I had to find out accidentally. You were never going to tell me it was you. You were never going to tell me about the baby."

"That's not true—"

"Isn't it? You had plenty of opportunities to tell me. When we were negotiating the sale of the estate, or maybe all the times since then. Why didn't you say anything?"

"Because, I—I was confused and worried. I don't really know you, Sebastian. I don't know if I can trust you."

"There's only one way to find out, Gracie," he whispered.

It was ironic and all backward. First, she'd had mind-blowing sex with him, then she'd conceived his child and now he wanted to date her.

"It's crazy."

"We do crazy well, Gracie."

His thoughts must've coincided with hers. They did do crazy well, starting with that night at the Texas Cattleman's Club masquerade ball, then Gracie finding a shirtless Sebastian by the pool, only to discover he was her mysterious lover. And then Sebastian finding out Gracie was carrying his child quite by accident.

She couldn't argue the point with him. She smiled. "True story."

He smiled back. "I'll pick you up at seven tomorrow

night." Then Sebastian opened the car door for her and she slid into her seat. After he gave a slight shove to close the door, she started the engine with the push of a button and drove off. A glance in the rearview mirror gave her one last look at hunky Sebastian Wingate.

Her date for tomorrow night.

Sebastian gave himself a dozen mental warnings before knocking on Gracie's door. He didn't want to blow it again by saying anything that would alienate her. Because the truth was, he desperately wanted to get to know her better, to see the woman behind the mask, per se. So far, all they'd done was argue, and he didn't want more of that. He'd have to walk on eggshells all night and not let his physical attraction to her get in the way of their date. Which meant he planned on being a perfect gentleman, even if it killed him.

He knocked and Gracie's housekeeper answered. Funny how the roles were reversed now. She had the servants and he was on the outside looking in.

The older woman let him in and then Gracie stepped into the foyer. Oh, man, it *was* going to kill him. She looked amazing, wearing a cinnamon-red hip-hugging dress that landed at her knees. Her olive skin peeked through the delicate red lace at the arms and back. Her hair, lustrous and long, teased her breasts. The night of the TCC masquerade ball, she'd also worn red, a shimmery gown that knocked him upside the head. He'd been drawn to her then, as he was now, the pull so strong he had no willpower around her.

Just last night he'd kissed her, tasted her lips again. It had been three long months of wondering, of trying to find his mystery woman, of not knowing who she might be. But that incredible kiss had brought back all the reasons why he couldn't get the woman in red off his mind. It hadn't been a fluke; it hadn't solely been about the forbidden thrill. It had been about the woman.

Gracie. Bold. Sexy. Unforgettable.

He cleared his throat. "You look…nice."

"So do you." Her response was automatic.

He'd spent extra time choosing his clothes. His slacks were pressed and he wore a shirt in deep purple, a color his mother called eggplant. But instead of a sports jacket, he wore a black suede bomber jacket. "Are you ready?"

She nodded, though she seemed hesitant and unsure. Beth had once told him that after winning the lottery, Gracie had been swarmed with male attention, and she could never be certain if the guys showed up for her or for her money. Though Gracie hardly knew how pretty she was, how sultry she appeared with that slender figure, those long legs and perfect breasts. Her eyes were large, expressive and black-coffee dark. Her skin was so smooth he hadn't forgotten how silky it felt beneath his palms.

But that was months ago, and now he had to show her a different side of him. He wanted to gain her trust and win her over. He wanted to be a part of their baby's life. His thoughts flashed to Lonny, and the role Sebastian had played in the young boy's life. Lonny was his ex-girlfriend's teenage brother, a boy deeply troubled, and

Sebastian had been there for him. He'd tried to give the boy his love and support, because heaven knew Lonny needed it. And he had for a time, but then Sebastian and his girlfriend had broken up and he'd lost touch with her younger brother. He'd always felt bad about not being there for the boy anymore.

Sebastian didn't want to let his own child down that way. He wanted to know his baby, be a positive influence in his or her life. He wanted so much not to screw up his child's life.

"Great, then let's get going. Do you have a coat? It's chilly outside."

"Yes," she said. "Right here."

She put on a knee-length sweater coat the same color of her dress and her distinct body language told him not to offer to help. It went against his instincts and the manners drilled into his head since he was a kid. But his mission tonight was to stay out of trouble and get to know her better.

He opened the door and they were hit with a blast of winter cold. "Ah," she said. "Smells fresh and clean out there."

She stepped outside and he waited for her to lock up the house. Then, without wasting another moment, he put his hand to her back and guided her to his black BMW. There was no question about him opening the car door for her. He went about it easily and she slid into the seat. By the time he got behind the wheel, she was belted in.

"I hope you like Italian."

She glanced at him. "Who doesn't?"

He laughed. "It's a bit of a drive, so sit back and relax."

"Where are we going?"

"Amore, just outside of town," he told her. "The chef is a friend, and he's very talented. Have you ever been there?"

"No, I don't think so. But it sounds good."

He winked. "I think you'll like it."

Gracie smiled in response.

"Care for some music or would you like to be quiet?"

"I wouldn't mind music," she said.

He clicked on the radio and Reba McEntire's powerful voice came through the speakers, singing along with Kelly Clarkson about pain and trust and hurt.

"I like this song," Gracie said, laying her head back against the headrest "It touches me with its truth."

Sebastian nodded. "Yeah."

Every second spent with Gracie taught him something new.

"Music tells the truth better than any other medium," she mused. "Don't you think?"

He'd never really thought about it before. "Could be. Maybe."

Gracie was touched by a song that spoke of heartache and mistrust. She was a cautious one, wary of involvements, as the song inferred. That much he knew about her, since she hadn't told him immediately about carrying his child. She'd been protective, and he was still

called The Eatery, in the heart of Royal," Sebas-
told him.

'Of course, the town's buzzing about it," Tony said.
re you a chef?"

"No, not me. My friend and associate, Lauren, is the
ulinary genius. I'm more the investor."

Tony eyed him briefly. He must've put two and two
ogether and recognized Gracie as the big Powerball
winner, but he was discreet enough not to mention it.
"Well, I'll have to visit your establishment one day and
see for myself."

"Please do," Gracie said with a sincere smile.

"If the chef's as talented as you say, then maybe I
should be glad your restaurant is across town."

"I think I'm glad, too," she said, charming the chef
into a grin.

"If you would allow me, I'd love to make you both a
special meal," Tony offered. "It would be my pleasure."

Sebastian glanced at her. "Is that okay?"

"Of course, that would be terrific, if it's okay with
you."

"Yeah, it'll be a treat." He gave Tony a nod. "Appreciate that, Chef."

"Shall I send over a bottle of our signature Amore
vino?"

Sebastian didn't have to think twice. "No, not tonight."

Gracie spoke up. "Please, don't let me stop you. If
you want a glass of wine, go ahead."

Sebastian shook his head. He wasn't about to drink

trying to get over her not revealing h[...]
she was confronted. Maybe he had trus[...]

Five songs later they were seated in [...]
ing room with a table set for two inside th[...]
"Thanks, Chef," he said to Tony Perrino. "T[...]

"Of course, anything for you, Sebastian."[...]
a silver fox, a sixty-year-old man who'd lived a[...]
times already and had finally settled in Texas[...]
had business dealings in the past and had deve[...]
friendship over golf and pasta through the years. [...]
wish you would let me feed you more often."

Sebastian turned to Gracie. "Gracie, this is my f[...]
Tony. He owns Amore. The only thing better than[...]
golf swing is his homemade pasta. He's bringing a li[...]
bit of the Old World to the Southwest."

Tony laughed and greeted Gracie with a bow of h[...]
head. "Pleasure to meet you, Gracie."

"Thank you. I love your place."

Gracie seemed to have an eye for design, and approval shone in her eyes as she scanned the small, intimate dining area. The restaurant spoke of European
elegance without being cliché or overdone. The table-
cloths were pristine white, the place settings hand-
painted Italian ceramic, the glassware cut crystal and
the centerpieces an array of pillar candles. There was
also a mini stage set up, where sometimes a band played
and sometimes singers entertained the patrons.

"It has so much charm," she said.

"I appreciate the compliment." The chef smiled.

"Gracie and a mutual friend just opened a restau-

wine when she couldn't have any. It would be that way for six months at the very least. "Thank you, Tony. But I'll pass."

Gracie studied him intently. "That was nice of you."

"I'm a nice guy."

Her brows went up, but she remained noncommittal. She didn't like to give an inch, but he was wearing her down. He could tell by her tone. It was much more gracious tonight.

"I hope you're hungry. You don't want to miss any of Tony's creations."

"My appetite is finally coming back. I had a little bout of morning sickness earlier in my pregnancy and had to force myself to eat. But I'm better now."

Sebastian looked away for a second and sighed. He'd have wanted to be there for Gracie and his child during that time. Maybe he could've helped out somehow. But that was water under the bridge now. There was no going back.

A server came by with a full basket of garlic knots. Gracie breathed in the aroma.

"Those smell soooo good."

"Try one."

"One? I may eat the whole basket, but since you're being nice, I'll save you one." She grabbed a piece of bread and began nibbling. "Yum... They taste as good as they smell."

And after they indulged in several, the server reappeared to present an eye-catching antipasto platter. Olives, artichokes, tomatoes and salami amid a variety of cheeses, all drizzled with olive oil over a nest of arugula and romaine lettuce.

Gracie looked impressed, because, well, Tony's creations were impressive. "I think I'm in heaven."

Sebastian looked her in the eye. "Really? Because of the company?"

"Yes."

He jerked back in his seat. Was this progress? Did she actually enjoy being with him?

"Chef Tony is pretty talented."

He shook his head. "Very funny."

"And this food is amazing."

She popped an olive into her mouth and his eyes followed the movement as she chewed delicately. Everything about Gracie moved him and made him hunger for more than food. "Well, at least I know you have good culinary taste. I'll check that box off."

"What other boxes are you planning on checking off with me?" she murmured.

That was a loaded question, but he'd opt for the safest bet. "I was hoping to get to know you better, Gracie."

"We've known each other a long time."

"Yes, but that doesn't mean we know things about each other. For instance, do you have hobbies? What was your favorite subject in school? Who do you admire most? Those are basics and yet I couldn't answer any of those about you."

She quirked a brow. "Would it matter?"

"It'd be a start."

"Horses, I love horses. I love riding, though lately I

haven't done much of it. Favorite subject, history. I like learning how we got to this point in our lives. There's so much still to learn. And as far as who I admire most? My father. He was a hardworking, honorable man. I miss him very much."

He liked the way her eyes lit up as she spoke of her father. She clearly loved and admired him a lot. Alberto Diaz was a good person. "Your dad was highly respected when he worked for us. Everyone remarked about how good he was with our horses. He was much more than a ranch manager. He had a special connection to the animals. It must be why you have such a fondness for horses."

"Maybe it's genetic, or maybe he taught me to love such regal animals."

"Could be a little bit of both," he said.

She smiled. "What about you?"

"Me? What about me?"

"Same questions."

"I like to ride, too. I have a great affection for all animals, but I've been around horses all my life, and they seem more human at times than the real thing."

"I know, right? What else?"

"I'd never refuse a round of golf, either. I take it as a personal challenge to better my game. I guess you could say those are my hobbies." He blew out a ragged breath. "But this year has been rough. I've spent most of my time trying to clear the family name and keep the company going. As you know, we were dealt a raw hand with Keith Cooper. That guy nearly destroyed Wingate, but we've been able to relaunch the hotel chain with a new brand and we've kept WinJet strictly in the US now. It's really helped our public image."

"Beth filled me in on some of it. I know it was tough on the family."

He nodded. It'd been all over the news, but the worst scandal was when the Wingate name was associated with drug runners. Thankfully, that was disproved pretty quickly. "Well, then you know the truth."

"I do, or I wouldn't be here right now."

"Fair enough."

"Go on. What's your favorite subject?" she asked.

"Gracie 101."

She shook her head and fought a smile. "Corny."

"Yeah, it was, but you did smile. A little."

That made her smile more and it was beautiful, as was seeing her eyes lighting up with pure, unabashed joy. She didn't smile enough around him.

"Okay, I'll be serious. Don't hate me, but math is my favorite subject. It comes easy to me, though Beth says it's a four-letter word. I remember tutoring her after school, but either you get it or you don't. I like that the answers are all there in black-and-white, and there are no gray areas."

"If only life was that simple," Gracie said on a sigh.

Somehow, he got the feeling they weren't talking about math anymore. Was she in a gray area in her life? She didn't have to be. He reached across the table and took her hand. She didn't flinch or pull away, but a quick gasp escaped her mouth when he lifted their entwined hands and brushed his lips across her knuckles. The connection sparked life between them. Made him want her more. "It can be, Gracie."

Skepticism touched her eyes. But the pull they had was real. He felt it sizzle through him. One touch and he was a goner.

"There's more to life than physical attraction," she said softly.

"That's very true, but it helps." Sebastian grinned and then tugged his hand away. He promised no pressure and he had to abide by that even as his body heated up from having her so irresistibly near.

The waiter brought over an array of dishes—pastas and eggplant and shrimp scampi. It was all beautifully arranged on several platters, more food than they could possibly eat in one sitting.

"Thank you," Sebastian said to the server.

Gracie took a look and opened her eyes wide. "I know I'm eating for two, but this is enough for a football team. It's amazing."

"I hoped you'd like it. Wanna dig in?"

She nodded. "I shouldn't. I've already eaten so much. But I've got to have a little taste of everything."

Sebastian refrained from helping her fill her plate. Gracie wasn't the wilting-flower kind of girl. He had to remember that. She helped herself and then offered to serve him. Since she already had a big serving spoon in her hand, he agreed. She was generous with her portions, giving him much more than he needed. He enjoyed watching her pick out items to set in his plate.

They ate quietly, Sebastian sipping lemonade, Gracie's drink of choice. It felt good being in sync with her, even if it was just by sharing food and drink. They spoke about her day at The Eatery and how the place had fared on the second day of business. The conversation was light, nothing too intense. And just doing these normal things together made him feel closer to her, closer to the baby.

A three-piece band walked onto the stage, and soon old Sinatra classics filled the dining room. The lead singer had a deep voice, his pitch-perfect tone catching the attention of everyone in the restaurant.

A few couples got up to dance. It was intimate and cozy, and the need to hold Gracie, if only for a few fleeting minutes, overpowered his good intentions. He rose from the table and offered her his hand. "Dance with me?"

Gracie glanced around the restaurant, as if measuring her options. Then she gazed at his outstretched hand and looked into his eyes. She sighed, as if losing a mental battle, and placed her hand in his.

He led her to the dance floor and took her in his arms, leaving a decent amount of space between them. It was harder than he thought, holding her and not drawing her close, not feeling her soft, supple body nestled up against his.

"Are you having a nice time?" he asked huskily.

She hesitated for a moment. "Yes."

Their eyes met then, and he nodded. "Good. Me, too."

"Is this another box you wanted to check off?"

"Dancing with you? I've thought about how we danced the night away at the ball so many times, and I can hardly believe we're doing it again. I was convinced I'd never find you," he whispered.

"You were shocked to find out it was me," she whispered back.

"Surprised, yes. But I was also glad it was you."

To his relief, Gracie began to slowly relax as they both found themselves swept up in the music. Her scent flavored the air around him, her body moved with rhythm and grace, and every so often, some part of her would touch him somewhere. Sebastian relished it all—her hair brushing his shoulder, her breasts grazing his chest, her legs teasing his thighs...

There was no doubt heat and desire had lodged between them, prickling his skin, making her skin flush. Like a slow-building fire, the longer he held her, the hotter it grew...until he felt a desperate, frenzied need to act on his impulses.

"Gracie," he whispered in her ear. And then she snuggled his neck and lifted her head up, locking her eyes with his. There was an openness on her face that he hadn't seen before, a sweet invitation.

He bent down and kissed her, a gentle tasting of her lips that sent him reeling. He had to remember where he was and stick to his promise to keep it chaste tonight. But she indulged in the kiss, keeping a tight grip on his neck as their lips brushed again. He wanted so much more from her. If only he could keep holding her and kissing her all night long. If only he could weave his fingers through her long, shiny hair, and inhale her delicious scent. If only he could make love to her again. Knowing full well who she was.

When the song ended, their eyes met again, searching, pondering and then silently acknowledging their incredible chemistry.

He cleared his throat. "Looks like Chef is ready to serve dessert," he said, as Tony came out personally with a dish of Italian pastries. "We shouldn't keep him waiting."

"Uh…no," she agreed, a little breathless. "We shouldn't."

He took her hand, leading her back to the table, and then greeted the chef again. The pastries were out-of-this-world appetizing. Yet, no matter how delectable the dessert, tonight nothing would match the taste of Gracie's lips on his.

# Four

After Sebastian walked her to her front door, Gracie put the key in the lock, realizing this was a pivotal moment for the two of them. If she invited him in, she was pretty sure what would happen. And she didn't know if she was ready for that. She didn't know if she could forgo all of her misgivings about getting romantically involved with him.

This date tonight was a chance to get to know each other better. It was a way to find out who they both were. She wasn't that mystery woman any longer. And he wasn't her mysterious lover. That fantasy was over; she now had to deal with the real-life Sebastian. Was he someone she could let into her life? Her child's life?

Tonight had been scary good. Sebastian had been

a perfect gentleman, except maybe for the kiss on the dance floor. She had to be honest with herself, though— it wasn't all his doing. She'd *wanted* him to hold her close, she'd wanted him to kiss her again. The emotion wrapped up in their encounter had been mind-blowing, so she couldn't fault him for something she'd subtly invited.

"I had a great time tonight," he said. "I hope you did, too."

She spun around to face him. Oh, boy, her fifteen-year-old self would hardly believe she'd actually gone on a date with Sebastian Wingate. That *he* was actually pursuing *her*. But she wasn't fifteen anymore. And things were different now.

"I did. It was…fun."

He nodded, his eyes gleaming. "I want to see you again."

She figured. And the idea wasn't making her stomach ache.

He went on, "What are you doing tomorrow?"

"I plan to be at The Eatery helping out. I'll be doing the books."

"Will it take all day?"

"Why?" she asked.

"Because I have something in mind. Can you clear up your afternoon?"

"I…think so."

"Great, I'll pick you up at two. And dress casual, although you do look amazing tonight." His gaze moved over her, a quick glint of approval, and a river of heat rushed down her body. "But tomorrow, just jeans and a jacket."

"Aren't you going to tell me what we're doing?"

"No, you're just going to have to trust me. Can you do that?"

She slanted him a look. "I'll…try."

"Great," he said, leaning forward and giving her a little peck on the cheek. "Sleep well, Gracie."

"You…too," she murmured, somewhat dumbfounded. But before she could utter another word, Sebastian had already turned away and was walking to his car.

So much for worrying about putting him off. She didn't know if that was a good thing or a bad thing. With Sebastian, her heart always warred with her head. But when it came down to their date, this was by far the best one she'd had…ever. But dating wasn't the issue. She worried about blurring the lines between her deep attraction to Sebastian and doing what was right for the baby. It was something that still confused her, still caused her ill ease.

Half an hour later, after she'd had a luxurious soak in the tub, her cell phone rang. She threw her arms into the sleeves of her cozy pajamas and picked up on the third ring. "Hello."

"Hi, it's Sebastian." The deep, sexy Texas drawl in his voice threw her off-kilter. Her heart began to pound. "Hi."

Was he calling to break their date tomorrow?

"Am I disturbing you?"

*Always.* Despite her caution and worry, she'd had

him on her mind all evening. Her body still hummed from their date—from dancing in his arms, from laughing with him and *kissing* him and secretly dreaming of so much more. "No, not at all. Just got out of the tub."

There was a long pause on his end. Dummy, why did she tell him that?

"I won't say what I'm thinking right now."

She chuckled. She deserved that. "Thank you."

"Gracie, as I told you earlier, I had a great time tonight. And well, I could make something up, a reason for the call, but the truth is, I just wanted to hear your voice one last time before I turned in. Hope that's okay."

She was taken aback by his sincerity. "Yes, actually that's very nice."

"I told you I'm a nice guy."

She paused. She knew it deep down in her bones, her instincts telling her so, but could she trust them right now? There was too much doubt and caution warring with the good stuff in her head. He could be charming, but he could also be quite ruthless. She wasn't forgetting his ploy to hold back the sale of the estate to get what he wanted. So no, she couldn't give him everything right now. A phone conversation, yes; other things, no. "You keep telling me that."

"Maybe if you hear it enough, you'll start to believe it."

She chuckled again. "So that's the strategy?"

"I wish I was that clever."

"You're not?" she asked.

"Not when it comes to you, Gracie. I'm actually a little...thrown off by you."

She felt the same way about him. Only, he'd been throwing her off for years. He'd never shown an interest in her or given her even a little reason to flirt. She'd grown to believe she wasn't in his league—he'd dated some high-profile women in the past—and had resigned herself to the fact that she just wasn't up to his standards. It'd hurt her and made her feel less worthy. And so all of this sudden adulation was hard to measure. "I could say the same."

"I never want to give you a reason to doubt me," he admitted gruffly.

She didn't know what to say to that. "Thank you," she whispered, for lack of a better answer. Yet, she did still have doubts. And one late-night phone call wasn't going to change that.

"Well, I'd better let you get some rest. Sweet dreams, Gracie," he said softly.

"Good night, Sebastian."

She had to admit, this man sure knew how to get what he wanted. He was chipping away at her resistance, slowly but surely.

Was he true-blue, or was it all a ploy to secure what he wanted?

Sebastian hung up with Gracie and sighed. He couldn't stop thinking about her, the way she'd looked tonight, how it felt to hold her tight in his arms. She was so pretty, but pretty wasn't enough. He was really trying to get to know her. She was the mother of his baby, for one. They both had an equal stake in this, but he wasn't going to deny Gracie had the upper hand. Slowly, she was letting him in. It wasn't fast enough for him; he wasn't a patient man. He wanted more than one night with her. But right now, that wasn't happening.

His cell phone rang and he glanced at the screen, puzzled to see his ex-girlfriend's name come up. "Hello."

"Sebastian? I'm so glad I reached you. I've been trying you for a few hours."

He'd shut his phone down during his date with Gracie, wanting no interruptions or distractions. "Hi, Rhonda. How are you?"

He hadn't seen Rhonda Pearson in over a year, but they texted from time to time. Her supermodel status had taken precedence over their relationship, and things hadn't worked out between them. But it had been an amical breakup. "I—I need your help, Sebastian. Can we meet somewhere?"

"Now? It's late. Can it wait?"

"It's about L-Lonny."

Sebastian's nerves rattled, hearing Lonny's name come up. There was desperation in Rhonda's voice. "What about Lonny?"

She was raising her fifteen-year-old brother all by herself, and the boy seemed lost at times, not having the stability a teen needed. Sebastian had taken to the kid, and the boy looked up to him. Not staying in touch with Lonny was one of Sebastian's biggest regrets. He'd planned to, but then Rhonda had thought a clean break would be better for the boy. Then Sebastian's business had gotten into trouble and suddenly he was persona non grata. So he'd stayed away.

"He's out of control. I don't know what to do with him. I just need someone to talk to, you know? He's always admired you. And well, you were really good with him."

"Rhonda, I can meet you tomorrow night. I wish it could be sooner, but I've got a full day of appointments."

"Tomorrow night is good. Thank you, Sebastian," she said gratefully. "I want to keep this as private as possible. You know my life's an open book, but not Lonny's. I don't want this to get out."

"It won't… I promise." Damn, Sebastian had always worried about the boy. He should've stayed in contact with him despite his business woes. Despite Rhonda thinking severing ties would be best. That boy needed direction and focus, and Sebastian had let him down. "Come to my office at eight o'clock and we'll talk. The place should be cleared out at that hour," he said.

"Okay. See you then, Sebastian. And thanks again."

The knock came precisely at two o'clock and Gracie was ready. She'd gotten home just twenty minutes ago and changed into a pair of skinny jeans. How long would she be able to wear them? Right now, the fit was perfect. She also wore a taupe ribbed sweater under a rust leather jacket and matching midlength boots.

She opened the door to Sebastian, who was dressed pretty much how she was—boots, jeans and a jacket over a tan shirt. He looked smoking hot. Her heart began to race and she mentally cursed. He hadn't said a word yet and she was already losing it.

"Afternoon, Gracie."

"Hi, Sebastian. You're right on time."

"Did you get your work done today?" he asked.

"Most of it. I brought some home to look at later." She gestured to her attire. "Do I…need anything else?"

"You look perfect, Gracie. I have what we'll need for the afternoon."

She scrunched her brows, suddenly not feeling so sure about this. "Are you going to tell me where we're going?"

He smiled. "You'll see. If you're ready, let's go."

She locked the door behind her and he led her to his BMW. A minute later, they were heading toward the Wingate, uh, the Diaz estate. "What're you doing?" she asked. She had no idea what he was up to.

"You are a curious thing, aren't you?"

"Yes, when my sanity is at stake."

"Believe me, you're going to like this. And no more questions. Deal?"

Was she ready to make a deal with Sebastian? She already had, really. She'd bought his house, and was having his child. What was one more? "Oh, all right. Deal."

He grinned, bringing the sexy lines around his mouth out to play. She turned away from him to look out the window. She didn't want him to know how much he tested her sanity, *for real*.

He bypassed the mansion and drove a little farther to stop at the stables. She gave him a long look.

"Horses," he said. "We both love them. How would you feel about a ride?"

"I would love it." Gracie hadn't been atop a horse in a long time. She missed it, and missed being around the stables. Technically, she was on her own property, though escrow hadn't gone through yet. But she'd promised not to displace the ranch horses and had kept on the wrangler and his one-man crew to oversee the stables.

"My horses are still here," Sebastian said. "Duke and Duchess."

"I know them. They're beautiful animals."

"I thought we'd give the royal pair some exercise, let them know they haven't been forgotten." It was also part of the sale of the house, that Sebastian could board his horses here until he could find another home for them. There were six other riding horses on the property, as well.

They got out of the car and walked over to the corral. Sebastian whistled, the sound perking up all the horses' ears, but it was Duke, the dapple gray gelding, and Duchess, the bay mare, who trotted over and hung their heads over the fence.

Sebastian patted them each between the ears, his low, deep voice resonating with the pair, who seemed to be taking his love and giving it right back. "Oh, hey, I've missed you two."

Gracie walked into the stable, filled a bucket with carrots and apples, just like she'd do when her father was working here, and strode back to the corral. Within seconds a huddle of horses began eating out of the palm of her hand.

"Well, look at you," Sebastian teased, "stealing my thunder."

"Food will win them over every time," she said, happy to be among the animals. It only reinforced her desire to one day breed and raise horses on the property.

"True," he concurred, walking over to her.

After the horses had their treats, Pete, the wrangler, walked out of the stable and greeted them. "Give me a minute or two, and I'll have them saddled up and ready to ride," he said.

Sebastian peered at her, and she nodded. "I think this time, Pete, we'll do it ourselves."

"Fine by me. I'll be in the office if you, uh, need me," he said, looking from Sebastian to her, perplexed. As if this whole arrangement was above his pay grade. She couldn't blame him. Things *were* a bit confusing around here, since she was the one signing his checks now.

After Pete walked off, Sebastian brought out both sets of saddles and tack, one at a time. Gracie hadn't forgotten how to get a horse ready to ride. She enjoyed every second of it, until it came time for her to lift the saddle onto Duchess.

"Whoa, there, Wonder Woman," Sebastian said. "I'll do the honors. This sucker is heavy."

Before she could say a word, Sebastian hoisted the saddle atop Duchess. She didn't mind one bit seeing his muscles bunch and his neck strain. There was something innately sexy about Sebastian in this setting.

Once the horses were saddled up, Gracie tried to slide her left boot into the stirrup, and as tall as she was, she still couldn't quite manage without a little help. Sebastian gave her rump a push up, his hand lingering a bit longer than necessary on her butt cheek. "Watch it, bud," she said lightly.

"Oh, I am. Trust me, I am."

Gracie peered into his twinkling eyes and shook her head at his shameless attempt at flirting. Once fully seated, she grabbed the reins.

"Something's missing. Give me a sec," Sebastian said.

He marched to his car and came back with two hats and a duffel bag. He mounted Duke and guided him toward Duchess. "Here you go," he declared, plopping a tan hat on her head. "Cute." Immediately, her eyes were shaded from the sun.

He didn't look *cute* in his hat. *Mesmerizing* was a better word, but then she'd always had a bias when it came to Sebastian. How often she'd gaze at him from a distance, the tall handsome Wingate twin saddling up his horse, riding out onto the land he owned. She'd often daydream about this very thing, riding out with him. And now here she was.

"What's in the bag?" she asked.

"Snacks."

She flashed him a grin. "Wow. You think of everything."

"This is our second date. There'll be no skimping."

"Good to know," Gracie said, making a clicking sound and encouraging the mare to get going, which Duchess did right on cue.

Sebastian caught up with her, and they were quiet for a while as the horses moved in sync with each other. She glanced over at him every now and then, watching as he took command of the animal, of the land. His jaw firm, his eyes focused, he made her jittery inside while the rolling landscape and beautiful scenery calmed her. The contrast wasn't lost on her, And yet, there was peace here. And sanity. She concentrated on that.

"How're you holding up?" he asked, breaking their silence.

"I'm loving this."

"I thought you would."

She quirked a brow. "And you knew this because of our conversation the other day?"

"Only partly. I used to see you with your dad, the joy on your face whenever you'd come back from a ride. I figured this might be something you'd enjoy."

"Those were good days," she admitted, feeling a little nostalgic. "I would look forward to those rides. They didn't happen often enough for me. Dad was a stickler about work, and only once he was caught up would I get to mount up with him. But oh, it was fun."

Sebastian smiled. "How adventurous are you feeling today?"

"Why?"

"There's something I want to show you. But it'll take us another thirty minutes to get there."

"And you're not going to tell me what it is?"

He thought about that a second. "It's a secret place I'd go with Sutton. There's an old shed my brother and I turned into a clubhouse. There's a running stream nearby. It's been years since I've been there. Don't know if it's still there. What do you say? Are you up for it?"

"Sounds like fun. Sure, I'm up for it."

"Great." Sebastian pointed west. "That way." He reined Duke in that direction and Duchess followed.

In less than thirty minutes, they reached a clearing, coming upon a rustic building erected several feet from the banks of a rushing stream.

"Would you look at that," he marveled, taking it all in. "It's still standing."

She imagined the twins playing in there as boys, laughing, raising a ruckus, telling scary stories. It wasn't a total wreck—the structure seemed relatively sound—yet the wood planks that served as protection from the elements were severely weathered. "It sure is."

The stream was gurgling, the water flowing by and catching sunlight. It appeared narrow enough to wade through on foot. Lush green trees beyond served as a verdant backdrop. It was truly a lovely spot.

"Let's dismount and check it out," he said.

He was off his horse quickly and then came around to Duchess. Gracie lifted her right leg over the saddle and held on to the saddle horn as she slid down the mare's left side. Sebastian caught her around the waist and guided her down the rest of the way, until her boots hit solid ground. She swallowed a deep breath as his hands applied slight pressure. He didn't back away…wasn't letting go. "Gracie," he whispered in her ear from behind.

Their connection sizzled, and as she turned around, she was fitted snugly in his arms. Hot desire arced between them. Her breathing grew heavy. There was a look of unmistakable hunger in his eyes. And when she lowered her gaze to his mouth, a rumbling groan rose from his throat.

At the sound of his restraint, something sparked within her. She couldn't figure out why all of a sudden she was okay with this, but she was. More than okay. Her body ached for him, for a release of the tension he provoked every time he walked into a room.

"Sebastian," she whispered.

And then his lips crashed down on hers, tasting, *devouring*, making her head swim in crazy delight. Beyond reason now, she pushed aside her misgivings. All she knew was that she wanted Sebastian.

Desperately.

Gracie poured herself into the kiss, tugging on his neck and squeezing closer to him. His body radiated heat and energy, warming every inch of her. Duchess shifted, becoming impatient, and stepped away from them, snorting. Her move left them both to realize they were out in the middle of a clearing, with no shelter other than a broken-down, cobwebbed clubhouse.

Sebastian hugged her to his chest for one last moment, then broke their connection, pulling away. "Seems Duchess has more sense than I do."

"Does she?" she asked.

"Don't tempt me, Gracie. This isn't easy."

"What's not easy?"

"You're gonna make me say it?" he rasped.

She nodded. She wanted to hear everything he had to say.

"I want your trust, Gracie. I don't want to mess this up by rushing you into anything. I lost my head for a moment, but more than anything now, I want to get to know you better. I want to build a bond with you."

"So you're on your best behavior?"

A sly grin crossed over his face. "You've already seen my best behavior."

"Ah," she replied, catching his meaning. The night of the masquerade ball immediately came to mind. The way he'd danced with her until they'd needed much more than casual touching. The way he'd whispered in her ear to leave the dance floor with him and the sizzling hot tingles that had her nodding her head. The way he'd made love to her that night had been nothing but the *best*. "But this is a close second?"

"Only if I'm winning you over. 'Cause believe me, if I had my way…" He shot her a hot glance that made her entire body twitch. She had no words.

He sighed and took her hand. "C'mon. Let's have something to eat."

He pulled a lightweight blanket out of the duffel and spread it a few feet from the creek. "Have a seat."

She sat cross-legged and he came down to face her.

She looked inside the bag and found all kinds of snacks. She helped him pull out a small loaf of bread and chunks of gourmet cheese, fresh apples, tortilla chips and two oversize chocolate cookies from The Eatery. "Hmm, I think I recognize these," she said, still tempering her heated body.

"Lauren's best," he murmured.

"I agree."

Together they munched on the snacks, Gracie totally aware of Sebastian. She liked the way he chewed, the way he swallowed, the way his eyes stayed focused on her even though there was beautiful scenery all around them.

"It's peaceful here," she said, taking a bite of the cookie.

"My brother and I would come here often when we were kids. It was our secret place, or so we thought. Turned out your father knew about it, too. We found out years later that he would come out here and make sure the building was kept up and solid, free of spiders and webs. Did he ever tell you about it?"

"No, never. But that sounds like something my father would do." She stared at the structure, picturing her dad making a point of stopping by every so often to make sure the boys were safe. "Dad was always good with horses, but he was also a softy when it came to children. Thanks for telling me, Sebastian. It makes this place special to me, too."

He nodded, giving her time to reminisce.

She appreciated that. No wonder she loved the estate; it was a part of her parents' lives as much as it was her own. She'd loved everything about the Wingate property—the land, the house itself. And now that she owned it, she realized there wasn't anything she wanted to change about the place. It was perfect. She'd always thought so.

When they were through eating, she started cleaning up and putting things back into the duffel bag.

"Are you ready to go?" he asked, a question in his eyes.

"Aren't you?"

He stood up and reached for her hand. "Take a walk with me?"

"Oh, uh, sure." Guess he wasn't ready to go, and honestly, neither was she. She was having a good time getting to know Sebastian better. As she placed her palm into his hand, he held it firmly in his grasp. There was something possessive in that gesture, which said, *You're with me.* It was thrilling and almost too good to be true. Did she deserve all of this good fortune? It was a question she often asked herself. It was hard for her to accept the way her life had changed, when in her heart she was still that same young girl who'd been on the outside, looking in.

They walked along the stream and she put her head on Sebastian's shoulder. It was a bold move, yet it felt right. He relaxed his shoulder and stopped walking to give her a delicious kiss.

It was perfect and easy and so natural.

"I'd love to see you tonight. For dinner," she added, surprising herself. When had the pursued become the pursuer?

Sebastian smiled, his eyes gleaming bright, but then his lips curled down into a frown as he seemed to remember something. "I'd love to take you up on that. But I can't tonight."

"Is it work?"

"A meeting. I'm afraid I can't get out of it."

He brushed a strand of hair from her cheek. That simple gesture and the caring look in his eyes moved her to distraction. "How about tomorrow night?" he asked.

"Yes," she said softly, immediately. "I accept."

He smiled, taking her hand, and they headed back to the horses.

Sebastian poured himself a rye whiskey from the small bar in his office. If he didn't have this meeting with his ex-girlfriend, he'd be with Gracie now and he'd be one step closer to getting what he wanted. He couldn't believe she'd actually asked him on a date.

And he'd had to refuse her.

Her trust was important to him, but he just couldn't bring himself to tell her about this meeting tonight. He'd promised Rhonda that he'd keep this meeting private. He understood her motives. She wanted to spare Lonny any more grief. The teen's problems didn't need to make the ten o'clock news. And Sebastian was a man of his word, so he'd told a little white lie to Gracie about what he was really doing tonight.

Rhonda Pearson, famous supermodel and his ex-lover, made headlines around the globe. Her photos had graced more than a dozen magazines, and she had a long list of accomplishments in the modeling industry. And all during that, she was trying to raise her much younger brother.

He took another swig of whiskey, and at precisely 8:00 p.m., he opened the door of the Wingate offices to Rhonda.

She smiled, but her eyes didn't reflect anything but sadness. "Sebastian, thanks for seeing me."

"Rhonda, come in."

He returned a smile, noting that his former flame hadn't changed since they'd dated. She was the same gorgeous, leggy blonde-haired beauty she'd always been. Rhonda had a natural grace about her, and yet, it hadn't been enough for him. She'd been too much in the public eye, too much into herself, to be the kind of woman he wanted. In the end, he'd allowed the press to believe she had called it off with him, so she could save face amid her fans. Sebastian had made the right decision in breaking it off with her. He hadn't once regretted their breakup, except for losing touch with Lonny. He'd been like a father to Lonny, a mentor of sorts, and then it had all ended. Sebastian hated that he hadn't fought harder to keep that relationship going.

He led her through the lobby and into his office. The staff had all gone home now, and he offered her a seat. She sat down on the sofa. "Care for a drink, something to eat?" he asked.

She glanced at his whiskey glass, not quite empty yet. "I'll have what you're having."

He lifted a brow and nodded. "That bad, uh?"

"That's why I'm drinking, but why are you? Is the company still having problems?"

He sighed as he walked to the bar to pour her drink. "Some. We're not fully out of the woods yet, but we're getting there. It's hard to gain back a reputation, you know?"

"I do know. That's why I try my best to stay away from scandal."

He poured whiskey into a tumbler and handed it to her. Then he took a seat at the other end of the sofa. "And yet here you are, in the sinful Wingates' den of thieves."

She chuckled at his theatrics. "I never believed it."

"That's what people say now that we've made it over the hurdle. But you're not here to talk about me. Tell me about Lonny."

And for the next half hour she filled him in on what was going on with her brother. Sebastian had always known that losing his parents at such a young age had affected Lonny, but now apparently it was causing the troubled teen to spin out of control. Rhonda told him Lonny was acting out whenever he could, getting in with the wrong crowd at school, to the point of almost being expelled. She had used all her powers of persuasion and superstar status to save him from the expulsion. The principal was giving her brother one last chance to change his ways—or face the consequences—and Rhonda was at her wits' end.

"I've already turned down more work than I've accepted, in order to be home more. If Lonny gets expelled, it'll be a black mark that will travel from school to school with him. He doesn't understand that, or he doesn't care. Either way, I have to do something with him. I threatened him with boarding school, and all he said to that was he always knew I wanted to get rid of him. Sebastian, I don't know what to do." She sipped her whiskey and sighed, tears welling in her eyes.

"You're not a bad sister, Rhonda," he said softly. She was just out of her element raising a young boy while trying to maintain a career. "As I recall, you put that boy first as much as you could. Has he seen a therapist?"

She gestured with her free hand, putting up fingers. "Three of them. He doesn't give an inch, won't open up. That's why I'm here, Sebastian. When we were together, he was the happiest I've seen him. He bonded with you."

"Yes, but he was younger then. I'm no therapist, but…"

"He'll listen to you. I *know* he will."

He shook his head. "No, that boy doesn't need a lecture."

"But will you try to talk to him, Sebastian? Will you come over and see him?"

Sebastian had a lot going on in his life right now, but he couldn't refuse helping a distressed young boy. Lonny just needed a chance—Sebastian knew that in his gut—and the way he'd let the boy down before still gnawed away at him. That was why he was so adamant about working things out with Gracie. He couldn't stand to lose another relationship with a child, *his* child this time.

His baby.

"I'll call you and set up a date. But it shouldn't look like we planned it. That'll turn Lonny off for sure."

"You mean we should accidentally run into each other?"

He nodded. "Something like that."

"Thank you," she breathed. "I feel better already." She put down her glass and rose. Sebastian took her elbow and walked her outside to where her car was parked. He opened the door for her, and before he knew what was happening, Rhonda kissed him, planting a grateful smack on his lips. Because he'd been with her for two years, he knew the difference between passion and gratitude. The kiss was purely innocent, but she'd landed it right out in the open. And a sudden pang of guilt hit him as Gracie's image came to mind, but he shoved that aside. The two situations, the two women, were totally different.

He glanced at his watch. It was quarter to nine. Not too late to visit Gracie.

He hoped not, because he didn't have it in him to stay away.

# Five

Gracie rubbed her backside, easing the soreness that lingered there from the ride on Duchess today. And even though she was paying a small price, the ride and the man had been perfect. She sighed. Sebastian had been open and honest with her as they spoke of their lives while growing up. They'd shared more about themselves on the ride and she'd laughed at some of the stories he'd told about his antics with his twin.

It seemed that in their youth, Sutton and Sebastian had a history of fooling people into believing one was the other. Teachers and friends had all fallen victim to their identical looks. And more recently, Lauren had been unintentionally misled that Sebastian had been the man she'd met during the masquerade ball, when it had really been Sutton. Once all was sorted out, Lauren and Sutton had fallen madly in love with each other.

If only she and Sebastian…

Gracie was just about to take the stairs when a knock at the front door startled her. Then her security alert chimed, and she glanced at the live feed on her phone.

Quickly, she fussed with her hair, straightened out her clothes and then opened the door to Sebastian.

"Hi," he said, charming her with a smile…and, well, his presence.

"Hi." Her heart pumped hard.

"I hope it's not too late to stop by. I wanted to give these to you," he said, and that was when she noticed a lovely bouquet of winter flowers in his hand.

He transferred the flowers to her. "They're beautiful," she murmured, bringing them to her nose for a sniff. Pine and cinnamon mixed with the sweet scent of roses, reminding her of the holiday just past.

"They're a thank-you for today. I had a good time."

"Yes, it was a nice day. Did your meeting end early?"

He hesitated a second too long and a part of her wondered if he'd been lying to her, though why he'd find the need wasn't quite clear. "It didn't take as long as I thought."

"Well, uh, would you like to come in?"

"It's not too late?" he asked.

She doubted she'd get any sleep tonight if she sent him away. "No, it's not too late." She opened the door wider and allowed him entrance.

He stepped into the house and turned to her. She

fingered a silky rose petal and smiled. "This way. I'll put these in water." She led him into the kitchen and set the bouquet down. As she reached up on tiptoes to get a vase from the cabinet, Sebastian was there behind her, lifting it off the shelf easily. He handed it to her. "Here you go."

She stared into his green eyes, those same eyes that had melted her and made her do crazy things, like shedding her clothes and making love with him in an alcove at the Texas Cattleman's Club. She nearly dropped the darn vase as that image revealed itself yet again. Could he tell what she was thinking? Were his eyes reflecting the same thoughts?

Sebastian took the vase from her and set it down, never once taking his gaze off her. He whispered, "Gracie," and she trembled from deep down and acknowledged what was happening. What she wanted to happen. "I swear I only came here to say thank-you."

"I know." The pull between them was powerful, and despite his motives, he was here and she didn't want him to leave. "I'm glad you did."

Maybe her hormones were out of whack. Or maybe they weren't. All she knew for sure was that she could no longer control herself around this man. She wanted to feel the same exquisite feelings she had before when Sebastian was simply a mystery to her. As she was to him. And maybe, just maybe, she liked the man she was getting to know, which, in turn, was adding even more fuel to their sizzling hot attraction. "Hearing you say that is music to my ears," he growled, wrapping one arm around her waist and bringing her up against him. The soft material of her skinny jeans pressed against his rougher denim as their bodies collided. Sebastian shook his head as if he couldn't help himself, as if not touching her was torture, and then brought his mouth to hers and kissed her until they both needed oxygen.

He cupped her head and kissed her again and again, each kiss stirring her up, making her hormones dance. Soon, her blouse was off, then his shirt. Their hands found skin, warm, inviting, the touching as fevered as their kisses. Sebastian's caresses destroyed her and she hungered for more…

He reached under her and she was lifted in his arms, his strength, the way he held her so effortlessly, the ultimate turn-on. She didn't mind this caveman act; she was like putty already and doubted she could walk. "Which way?" he rasped, between kisses.

"Up the stairs, to the right," she said breathlessly. "Hurry."

Sebastian groaned as he kissed her again, making his way up the staircase. Her big bed loomed large in the room. He lowered her down upon it and she lay there quietly as he removed her clothes. "Hot," he remarked about her cherry-red underwear, taking precious care with her bra and then sliding the panties down her thighs slowly, savoring every second. She was naked and so damn sexy he could barely breathe.

"I never saw you like this, Gracie. You are so beautiful." The last time, it'd been too dark to see much, and they'd only gone by feel. But tonight was very different.

"My turn," she said softly, rising up from the bed with a smile. She pulled the zipper of his pants down and helped him kick them off. Next came his boxers and then he was bared to her. She laid her hand on his shaft, stroked him and then put her mouth on him. His knees nearly buckled under him. He loved Gracie's confidence, her unbelievable boldness, but it was almost too much. *Almost.*

And when she was through, he offered her the same, grazing the apex of her thighs with his tongue, his hand. Mattress sounds didn't rival Gracie's moans of pleasure as he brought her to utter completion. He loved that she didn't hold back, didn't hide her enthusiasm. Her whimpers in the aftermath bolstered his ego. When her breathing slowed, he pulled her into his arms. "We haven't even gotten to the good part yet," he whispered wickedly in her ear.

She chuckled and folded her body closer into his, her long, thick hair teasing his sensitized skin. It hadn't been a fluke the last time. It hadn't been just the thrill of the unknown. Gracie was the best lover he'd ever had. And he wondered about other men in her life. How many? Who? Had it been this great with them? He didn't want to think about Gracie with other guys. Twinges of jealousy surfaced. He'd never felt this way before. Not with Rhonda or any other woman.

But those thoughts were short-lived. Their night was not over yet. And when he made a move toward Gracie, she shook her head. He had a moment of panic at her refusal, until she climbed atop and straddled him. Staring up at her, with her olive skin glistening in the moonlight and her lustrous hair falling gloriously past her shoulders, he felt completely spellbound by this woman. Man, oh, man, how had he managed to keep away from her all these years?

"Sebastian," she said softly as she came down onto him, squeezing her eyes closed, giving him an unforgettable image of her naked beauty making love to him. He gritted his teeth as she moved slowly up and down, setting a sensual pace and rocking him to his very core. When it became too much to take, he grabbed her hips and their eyes met as he sped up his thrusts. She followed his beat, his rhythm, the bounce of her body exquisite to watch. Then her mouth gaped open, her breathing hitched and her eyes shuttered as her release washed over him. The beauty of that moment shattered him completely, and he couldn't hold back another second. He experienced the best damn orgasm of his life.

Afterward, they lay quietly in bed for a while, both staring up at the ceiling. "Was it—"

"Yes," she said. "Now we don't have to wonder anymore."

"You wondered, too?"

"Of course, I did," she admitted. "I've never made love with a stranger before. I'm not usually that…wild."

"I like wild. But you're not?"

"No. Not even close."

"So it must mean something."

"It means we have great sex," she whispered.

"Right." They did. So why was he disappointed in her answer? Why was she still wary of him? Still unwilling to admit they had more than great sex.

He stared at her abdomen, the place where his baby was growing and thriving. He wanted so much for that child. But he didn't want to press his luck with Gracie, either. He took hold of her hand, entwining their fingers. "Be my date for Cam and Beth's wedding."

He was going to be the man in Gracie's life. And it wasn't all about the baby. It was her and the way he was beginning to feel about her. He waited for her answer, and finally, after she was quiet for several seconds, he asked, "Is that a problem?"

She rolled over to face him. "It's just that people will think…"

"That I'm the baby's father?"

"No… Yes."

It stung that she didn't want people to know the truth about the baby. Sebastian was ready to let the world know. He didn't like lying to his family this way, or at the very least, omitting the truth from them. He wanted Gracie, but she was still gun-shy.

"It's just that…I'm not ready. I don't know where this is heading and I don't want to explain the situation to everyone, when I don't, uh, *we* don't, have answers."

He had answers, but she didn't want to hear them right now. "You're going as my date. It's as simple as that," he said. "No one's going to presume anything, or even if they did, I doubt they'd ask you."

Eventually, everyone would find out the truth. He was going to play a role in the baby's life, that was a given. Gracie couldn't keep his paternity secret much longer—he had rights, too, and he wasn't going to back off. That said, he was trying to give her some latitude here, by not putting undue pressure on her. But he did want to bring her to the wedding.

*To stake your claim,* said the little bug in his ear. Having her on his arm would be a step in the right direction. "I'd love to take you," he said, stroking her arm up and down.

She laid her head on his chest. "Okay, then, yes," she whispered.

"You'll go with me?"

"Yes, I'll go to the wedding with you."

He nodded. Finally, he'd have a chance to get to know Gracie a little better. To find out if what they had that night was real. He wanted her, but he also wanted to discover what made her tick.

Gracie woke to the sound of Sebastian's light breathing. It was dawn or a short time after, she couldn't tell. She was still in a daze about what had happened between them last night. She glanced at him sleeping next to her in bed, his broad muscled body that had worked magic on her now relaxed in sleep. Making love with Sebastian was unequaled, she didn't doubt that. But she could easily let him into her heart, and that was what scared her. She wanted to, so badly, but her instincts told her not to go all in with him. Life wasn't so neat and tidy that she'd have all of her fantasies come true. A man she'd always wanted, a baby she already loved and riches beyond her belief. At some point, this merry-go-round would stop to let her off.

She still had doubts in her mind about Sebastian. Even after last night. Physically, they were in tune, but what about everything else?

The bed creaked as she tossed off the covers and rose, stretching out her arms. She walked into the bathroom quietly and turned on the shower. Stepping inside, she shivered from the chill in the January air, until the hot spray rained down, spreading a delicious warmth. She'd had a workout last night, too, and she welcomed the heat that soothed her muscles.

When the glass door opened with a click, she spun around. Sebastian stood naked behind the door, a devilishly charming smile on his face. "Mind if I join you?"

Another fantasy coming true. Was she dreaming, or was this as real as it got? "Come in, the water's perfect."

He stepped inside. "You're the one that's perfect." He laid a hand on her tummy. Was there a little bump emerging? "So is this little one."

He kissed her then, under the hot spray of water. And then his hands were on her, soaping her up, touching her in private places, sliding seductively over her swollen breasts. She trusted him with her body, and so far, she hadn't been disappointed.

She kissed him back, using the bar of soap to lather him up good. And when she was just about done, and the lather was washed off, his large hands came around to her rear end and he lifted her slightly onto him. She tucked her legs around his waist, fully secure in his grip. There was no doubt this was going to happen again. She'd known it the second the shower door clicked open, but the intensity of their lovemaking always surprised her. Her heart beat fast, her body heated up, the water lapping over them giving her a thrill. He held her tight, moving deeper inside, taking the burden of the thrusts upon himself. It was too passionate, too torrid, and she couldn't hold on another second. She gripped his neck and spun out of control, her release mind-blowing.

Their lovemaking was raw and beautiful, just like the two times before. With no worries about the actual act, since she was already pregnant and they'd both confessed to not having any prior physical relationships for a long while, she harbored no regrets. Sebastian kissed her again and then shut off the water. They held each other for long moments, regaining normal breaths and coming back down to earth.

"Do you like bacon and eggs?" she asked him.

He chuckled. "That's the last thing I thought you'd say right now."

"The baby needs to eat. And it'll be egg whites and turkey bacon, but I make a mean omelet if you're hungry."

"I accept." He kissed her nose, and it was the simple things like that that captivated her. "Only if you let me help."

"Can you make coffee?"

"Of course," he answered.

And twenty minutes later, they were dressed and working in the kitchen, the flowers he'd given her last night adorning the center of the kitchen table. It was a cozy scene, a fact that didn't escape her as they went about making breakfast together.

Another one of her youthful imaginings coming to life.

But that was fantasy and this was real.

She didn't for a minute know how long it would last.

Gracie walked into The Eatery later that morning and greeted Lauren in the kitchen. Her business partner was hard at work, developing her special of the day, basil herb chicken with roasted vegetables. "Smells good in here."

"As it should," Lauren said, putting the finishing touch on the dish with a drizzle of extra-virgin olive oil. She looked the part in her uniform jacket and toque blanche, as she called her chef hat, a historical name from years gone by.

"Looks like word is spreading. We've got a decent lunch crowd."

"Yep, some of my regulars from Street Eats are coming in and helping spread the word," Lauren replied. "We're busy, which makes me extremely happy."

"Oh, I thought Sutton was the only one who could do that."

"Very funny! Good food and a good man rank up there on my happy scale. And you should talk… Sutton tells me Sebastian didn't come home last night. Which may very well explain the healthy glow on your face."

Was it that obvious? "It's amazing what prenatal vitamins can do."

"They can only do so much, Gracie."

"And how would Sutton know about Sebastian's comings and goings? I thought he spent his nights with you."

"He goes home every once in a while, to water the plants." She winked.

"You're so bad."

"It's okay if you don't want to tell me." Lauren feigned a pout.

Gracie didn't want anyone to know about her budding relationship with her baby's daddy. But Lauren was a good friend, and she knew about the night of the masquerade ball. She supposed if she told anyone, it would be her business partner. "Maybe Sebastian and I went on a date, and maybe he just stopped by last night to bring me a bouquet of flowers."

"Sounds interesting. Go on."

She rolled her eyes. "Can't you use your imagination, Chef?"

"I do, with my creations, but when it comes to friends, I want to hear it all."

"Okay, fine. Since I need a favor from you, I'll tell you that Sebastian made me happy twice last night."

Lauren's eyes bugged out. "Wow," she mouthed. "That's awesome. Are you two…"

"Dating? Sort of. He's taking me to Beth and Cam's wedding. And I don't know what the heck I'm doing."

"You don't have to know, Gracie. Just let things happen naturally."

"I don't want to be pressured, that's all," she admitted.

"Sebastian knows that, I'm sure. But it would be absolutely per—"

"About that favor," she interrupted. She knew it would be perfect if Sebastian fell in love with her, but that might not ever happen, and she had the baby to protect. For as hard as she tried, she couldn't shake off the constant, nagging suspicion that she'd never been good enough for a Wingate, and that was why Sebastian had never even considered her an option. But no matter what, she wasn't going to settle for anything less than true love. She wanted the kind of love that made birds sing and flowers bloom.

She wanted the fairy tale.

"When it slows down in here, will you help me shop for a dress for Beth's wedding?" she asked.

"I'd love to. Give me two hours to serve the lunch crowd and I'll go with you."

"Great, I'll plant myself in the back office and do some work until you're ready."

Lauren dug her teeth into her lower lip. "You know, you already have a gorgeous red gown."

Gracie began shaking her head. "No way. I can't go in the dress I wore to the masquerade ball, Lauren. Not anymore than you can." They'd both worn deep red gowns and gold masks on that night, part of the reason there'd been a case of mistaken identity.

"I know." Her friend shrugged. "It was just a thought."

"If you need me for anything, just give a shout. I'll be in the back."

And three hours later, Gracie and Lauren walked into a high-end boutique in Royal and, with the help of a very astute saleswoman, narrowed down Gracie's choices to three. In between try-on sessions, they were served passion fruit herbal tea and cookies. Both passed on the cookies but sipped the tea. Gracie and Lauren both came from humble beginnings, and this type of not off-the-rack shopping was new to them. But it was fun, and Gracie felt a little bit like Julia Roberts in *Pretty Woman* choosing a dress this way. Only, she was using her own credit card for the purchase.

The saleswoman, Edith, couldn't be nicer, even though Gracie opted for a dress on clearance that was slightly more money than she'd earn as a waitress for a month. "It's fabulous on you," Edith said.

"I think it's the one, Gracie," Lauren concurred.

Gracie glanced at herself in the triple mirror, admiring the amethyst lace dress from all angles. It had off-the-shoulder sleeves, a sweetheart neckline decorated with delicate rhinestones that traveled down to a tapered waistline and a high-low hem hitting her well below the knee. She knew it might just be the last time she'd squeeze into a garment like this. Her tummy was still flat, but her breasts were fuller and her waist was thickening a little. All in preparation for the baby, so it was a good thing. "I think so, too."

"Wonderful! Shall I get it ready for delivery?" Edith asked.

Gracie looked to Lauren, and she nodded enthusiastically.

"Yes, I think so."

"Great! If you don't mind me saying so, I'm thrilled to have met you, Miss Diaz. To think Rhonda Pearson came in just before you. Two celebrities in just one day."

"I'm hardly a celebrity," Gracie said, humbled. "So Rhonda Pearson shops here, too?" She knew Rhonda had dated Sebastian for a long time. Rumor had it they were to be married, but then they'd had a very public breakup. The supermodel had dumped him and the tabloids had a field day with that story. Now Rhonda was back in town. To see Sebastian?

"Why, yes, she does. She has excellent taste in clothes, if I do say do myself. And why wouldn't she? She's an international supermodel and just a lovely person."

"Y-yes, I suppose she is, though I've never met her," Gracie said.

Rhonda was gorgeous, from high cheekbones and perfect bone structure to a sweet-as-sugar smile. Plus, she had a mane of stunning blond hair that any woman would envy.

Gracie wasn't going to lie to herself, she didn't like the memories flashing in her head of Rhonda and Sebastian. They'd made headlines often. And maybe a streak of jealousy flitted through her system, as well as self-doubt. She's never been in Sebastian's league, and Rhonda Pearson could make even the most confident woman feel the lesser.

She tried not to think about it, yet feelings of unease still wedged their way in.

"Thanks for the tea, Edith," Lauren said. "And for your help today. I'm afraid I have to get back to work. Gracie and I just opened The Eatery in town. Perhaps you've heard of it? We'd love it if you stopped by one day, and be sure to bring your family."

Edith smiled warmly. "Thank you. I certainly will."

Gracie changed into her street clothes and handed the dress back to Edith. "Thanks again."

"Sure thing. I'll have it sent to your home by tomorrow."

"I appreciate that," she said.

"All part of the service." Edith beamed. "And thanks for shopping at Goodwins. Goodbye, now."

Lauren took Gracie's arm and ushered her outside. "That was a blast! I like spending your money, Gracie. Does that make me a terrible friend?"

"I don't think of it that way, Lauren. We're friends and *partners*, so in a way you're making me money."

"Okay, I'll take that. And OMG that dress—it's stunning on you! Sebastian won't know what hit him. The only trouble is, now I have to find something to knock Sutton's socks off."

"Lauren, you're engaged to him, and he thinks the sun shines on your shoulders. You have no worries."

# FREE BOOKS GIVEAWAY

Complete the survey below and return it today to receive up to 4 FREE BOOKS and FREE GIFTS guaranteed!

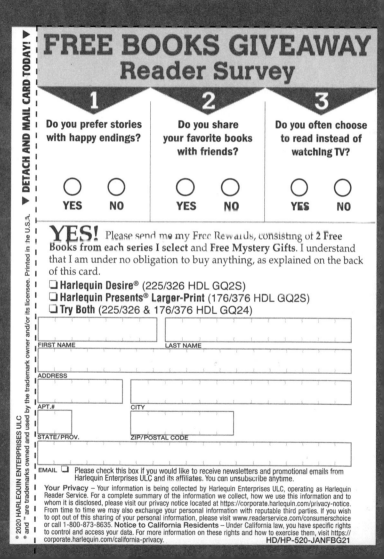

▶ DETACH AND MAIL CARD TODAY!

# FREE BOOKS GIVEAWAY
## Reader Survey

**1**

Do you prefer stories with happy endings?

○ YES  ○ NO

**2**

Do you share your favorite books with friends?

○ YES  ○ NO

**3**

Do you often choose to read instead of watching TV?

○ YES  ○ NO

**YES!** Please send me my Free Rewards, consisting of **2 Free Books** from each series I select and **Free Mystery Gifts**. I understand that I am under no obligation to buy anything, as explained on the back of this card.

❑ **Harlequin Desire®** (225/326 HDL GQ2S)
❑ **Harlequin Presents® Larger-Print** (176/376 HDL GQ2S)
❑ **Try Both** (225/326 & 176/376 HDL GQ24)

FIRST NAME | LAST NAME

ADDRESS

APT.# | CITY

STATE/PROV. | ZIP/POSTAL CODE

EMAIL ❑  Please check this box if you would like to receive newsletters and promotional emails from Harlequin Enterprises ULC and its affiliates. You can unsubscribe anytime.

**Your Privacy** – Your information is being collected by Harlequin Enterprises ULC, operating as Harlequin Reader Service. For a complete summary of the information we collect, how we use this information and to whom it is disclosed, please visit our privacy notice located at https://corporate.harlequin.com/privacy-notice. From time to time we may also exchange your personal information with reputable third parties. If you wish to opt out of this sharing of your personal information, please visit www.readerservice.com/consumerschoice or call 1-800-873-8635. **Notice to California Residents** – Under California law, you have specific rights to control and access your data. For more information on these rights and how to exercise them, visit https://corporate.harlequin.com/california-privacy.

HD/HP-520-JANFBG21

Printed in the U.S.A.

® 2020 HARLEQUIN ENTERPRISES ULC
® and ™ are trademarks owned and used by the trademark owner and/or its licensee.

# HARLEQUIN READER SERVICE—Here's how it works:

"I know." She giggled and kept the smile on her face all the way back to The Eatery.

Sebastian straightened his charcoal-and-black paisley tie in the mirror. He couldn't believe his sister Beth was getting married today. Cam Guthrie was a good guy, a hard worker and a man who'd been building Beth a dream home on property that was intended to be their working dude ranch resort. They were getting married in a private family ceremony today and Gracie was going as his date.

"What're you smiling about?" Sutton poked his head into the room.

"Beth," he lied. "She's the happiest I've ever seen her."

"So are you lately. Must have something to do with a certain pretty woman we both know."

"Maybe." He glanced at his brother. "But for years while growing up, Gracie wasn't someone I thought I could date or even think of that way. She's a little skittish around me, too, so we'll see how it goes tonight."

"Got it. But otherwise things are going well?"

He nodded. He didn't want to go into detail, so he kept his mouth shut.

"Hey, I have some news," Sutton said. "Not to put a damper on the day, but you should know about this. Chloe had a hunch about Keith Cooper's involvement when Dad was recovering from his stroke. She thinks that while he was supposedly *helping out* with the company, he might've dipped his hand into the till, too.

Miles is doing some digging now. And you know our brother—he won't rest until he finds out the truth. He wants us to sit tight and see what he comes up with."

"If anyone can sort through the BS, it's Miles." Chloe was Miles's fiancée and both were delving into the family's past finances.

Sebastian scratched his chin. What a corrupt man Keith Cooper had turned out to be. "It's not the kind of news we want to talk about at the wedding."

"No, I agree. But I wanted to keep you up-to-date."

"Got it," Sebastian said. "We'll just wait to hear what Miles finds out."

"Right. But in any event, this is gonna be a happy day. The family needs a fun celebration to remember what life was like before all the negativity and deception."

Sebastian glanced at his watch—it was almost time to pick up Gracie. His heart thumped hard, a current familiar reaction whenever he thought about her. This date was more than a date, because it was Beth's wedding, and both he and Gracie loved her, wanted to see her happy. They had that in common. But for the first time, the family would see Gracie on his arm. He wanted that. He wanted to step up instead of hiding his paternity. Maybe today would be a start toward making that happen.

"Time to run, bro," he told Sutton.

"Yeah, me, too. I'm picking up Lauren in a few minutes. Can't wait to see the house, now that it's all finished. Should be a special night."

He slapped his brother on the back. "And not just for Cam and Beth, but for all of us."

A short while later, Sebastian stood on Gracie's threshold in total awe, mesmerized by the smile that lit up her entire face. The dress she wore was a knockout, fitting her form perfectly. Its deep amethyst color highlighted her olive skin tones and the smoky brown of her eyes. Her hair was up in a do that looked both complicated and trendy, held together by a rhinestone clasp in the back.

"You look…" Delicious. Gorgeous. Stunning.

"Thank you. You look nice, too. Let me just get my coat. Come in."

He stepped into her foyer. She was back with a cream-colored faux fur coat and a clutch purse. As he helped her put it on, the delicate scent of flowers tickled his nostrils. "Love that perfume," he whispered as he tucked her into the coat, holding her lapels tight. "Reminds me of the other night." *When they'd made love…*

"You mean the way I smelled after getting off Duchess." She sent him a coy smile.

"Right, that's exactly what I meant." He tilted his head and leaned in to brush a quick kiss to her lips. It was something he needed to do, for his own sanity. He'd have to be a perfect gentleman tonight, in front of his family, and that was plain no fun.

"We should go," he said softly, stealing one more kiss. "Sorry, that's gonna have to hold me through the night."

It was getting harder and harder to keep this slow pace with Gracie. He'd never been a patient man, and his baby mama was testing his limits.

# Six

Gracie had seen the plans for the renovation of the two-story house, but nothing compared to seeing it in person. As Sebastian drove up, the entire ranchland was spread out before them, and smack in the center was Cam and Beth's glorious home constructed with river stone, an amazing glass-and-wood double-door entry and a red tile roof. The architecture, a harmonious mix of Spanish style and Craftsman, spoke of casual elegance. The first floor had a wide veranda that could probably hold every single guest at the wedding, while the second floor sported a wraparound balcony, and she could only imagine the view from there on a clear blue-sky day.

There were also bunkhouses and outer buildings

and a gorgeous redone barn painted the color of fresh meadow grass.

The invitation said cocktails in the main house first, before the ceremony, but the actual wedding would take place in the barn. It was Cam and Beth's way of holding an open house as well as a wedding. Sebastian turned his keys over to a valet and waved the attendant off, opening the door for Gracie himself.

He took her hand and led her up the steps of the grand home. Inside, they explored the rooms, checking out a dining room set with a large pine finished table and enough seating for ten. The great room was just that, *great* and large, furnished with an array of bulky furniture toned down by Beth's soft, feminine touch. Gracie's eyes drifted to the stone fireplace, which captured the room's essence, floor-to-ceiling and massive, but again was not overdone, as a mantel displayed family photos backlit by pillar candles. Beth and Cam had good insight into making this space homey and comfortable.

Waiters came by offering champagne and appetizers, and Gracie was touched when Sebastian took two flutes of sparkling water instead, offering her one with a smile. Seeing the food, her stomach growled, and she had no trouble accepting bacon-wrapped shrimp and a mini beef Wellington from another server. Sebastian watched her eat, his gorgeous green eyes on her as she chewed with gusto.

They spent time admiring the house, and then Harley and Grant spotted them and walked over with little

Daniel. "Hi, you two," Harley said, giving them both quizzical looks. Grant, too, seemed surprised at seeing the two of them together. He was the doctor who'd been helping her with hormone therapy so she could have an in vitro procedure.

Sebastian gave his sister a kiss on the cheek. "Harley, you look very pretty tonight." He shook Grant's hand, and then patted Daniel's head. "Hey, buddy, how's my favorite nephew today? Excited for Aunt Beth's wedding?"

"Uh-huh." The four-year-old bobbed his head up and down. "And cake."

They all laughed. "I bet your mom will let you have as much cake as you'd like tonight."

"Well, I wouldn't go that far." Harley gave her brother a quelling look.

Sebastian smiled at the boy. "Daniel, can you say hello to my girlfriend, Gracie?"

Daniel looked at her with big innocent eyes, while Harley and Grant exchanged glances. She'd never thought of herself as Sebastian's girlfriend, yet it sounded right, and she wouldn't refute it. "Hi, Daniel. I like your bow tie. You sure look handsome today. Maybe you and I can have a dance later on."

Daniel wiggled his nose, as if that was an awful idea. "May…be."

Harley took her hand and pulled her into a warm embrace. "Hi, Gracie. It's pretty cool that you're dating my brother now."

"Yes, we've, uh, been on a few dates." She turned to Dr. Everett. "Hello. Nice to see you again."

"Hello, Gracie. It's good to see you, as well," he said discreetly. He was her doctor, and he must know that she'd gotten pregnant the natural way, since she hadn't gone through with the in vitro.

"Grant and I have some news," Harley said. Her eyes beamed bright and eager, as if she couldn't contain herself. "I'm not going to make a big deal of this, since it's Beth's big day, but we've decided to leave for Thailand in two weeks. We're anxious to get started on our work overseas. We just can't wait. We've told Daniel, and he's excited about having this grand adventure."

"Wow, that's pretty quick," Sebastian said. "I'm sure you'll do a lot of good over there. But we're really gonna miss you."

"Thanks. And we'll miss you all, too." Grant put his arm around Harley's shoulder and drew his son in close. "But now is the right time for us to go."

Gracie thought their commitment to go to a foreign land to bring change to the health care of the underprivileged was such a selfless and generous undertaking.

The rest of Sebastian's siblings and their significant others circled them, along with other relatives—Miles and Chloe, Sutton and Lauren, Piper and Brian, Luke and Kelly, and Zeke and Reagan. Once again Sebastian took her hand and made sure she was included, as his date and family friend, as they wished Grant and Harley good luck on their travels.

Right after, it was announced that the ceremony was

about to begin, and everyone filed outside and headed to the barn.

As she and Sebastian stepped inside the wide doors, they entered into a wedding winter wonderland. Beth had done much of this by herself, and Gracie was honestly floored by what she'd accomplished, transforming a large, rustic barn into every bride's dream. Half of the barn was set up for the ceremony, and the other half with tables and chairs ready for the reception. They walked toward their seats, separated by a snowy white aisleway.

"Wow," she said. "Beth has outdone herself here."

Sebastian gazed around and nodded, "Yes, she has."

Above them, sheets of sheer fabric swooped down from the rafters, and twinkling lights overhead softly illuminated the entire barn. Candles centered pedestals and were surrounded by greenery and red roses. The chairs were gold, with big ivory bows wrapped around their backs. It was a small private wedding with only family and close friends in attendance, and all thirty of the guests had admiring eyes as they took their seats.

Gracie was thrilled for Beth, who deserved every bit of this happiness with Cam, the widower rancher. They would have a good life together. Gracie sighed, and Sebastian picked up on it. "What is it?"

"Nothing."

His brows rose. "No? Sounded like something."

"It's just all so beautiful. I'm happy for Beth and Cam."

"So am I." He stared at her for such a long moment

that she had to turn away. Because she saw something in his eyes that worried her, something that said they could have this, too. But no, Sebastian didn't love her, and that was her bottom line. After the love and trust her parents shared, and now her good friends Lauren and Beth had found, how could she settle for anything less? How could she trust what she herself was feeling? Aside from her hormones acting up, she had pregnancy brain. It was a real thing, her friends had told her, and along with it came muddled confusion. She was beginning to believe they were right.

Gracie returned her focus to the decor and the detail Beth had put into transforming the barn. It was a much safer thing to think about. Weddings made her sentimental, and she was a big fat softy when it came to seeing a groom up at the altar awaiting his bride.

When the music from a three-piece orchestra began, everyone rose and turned. And there was Beth, her smile shining, rivaling the sparkling lights. She looked gorgeous in an understated ivory gown that flowed Cinderella-like around her. Whispered oohs and aahs from the guests filled the room. Beside Beth stood her mother, Ava, the matriarch of the family. Someone who had issues with all of her children, it seemed, but in light of recent events, was trying to make amends. She was dressed in azure blue, her thick silver hair down in a flip, the lines in her face softening as she began her walk down the aisle next to Beth. It was an olive branch to her family, a way to show them she had their backs from now on.

Cam looked handsome in a black tuxedo and bolo tie. The good-looking rancher was the ideal match for Beth. They spoke vows to each other solemnly, but not completely void of humor. Through tears and laughter, they became husband and wife.

Sebastian squeezed her hand when the newly married couple turned to each other and sealed the deal with a kiss.

Gracie's eyes were watering, and Sebastian was there, handing her a handkerchief. She dabbed at her eyes, and then, as the minister pronounced them Mr. and Mrs. Guthrie, she applauded along with the others.

A little later on, Gracie met up with Cam and Beth at the receiving line. "Congratulations, you two!" She hugged Beth first, then Cam. "It was a beautiful ceremony."

"Thank you." Beth's eyes were misty, too. "It went just as I'd hoped."

"It sure did! And I couldn't be happier for you."

Sebastian was only a step behind, giving hugs out to his sister and shaking Cam's hand. "Good luck and congrats. Sis, you look amazing." He kissed Beth's cheek. "Love you."

"Love you, too."

Sebastian took Gracie's hand then, holding her possessively, and Beth's eyes widened. "Did you two come together?"

"Yes," Sebastian was quick to say. "We came together."

Beth's gaze met hers, and her look said, *We have to*

*talk later.* She did owe her friend an explanation, but now was not the time. "Well, it's about time you dated someone we all like," Beth told her brother.

Sebastian only smiled and led her away. They found their dining table, one of six decorated with white linens and golden utensils. A mini chandelier hung above each of the tables, providing sparkling light overhead, and winter sprigs laced with deep red roses made for a lovely centerpiece.

"What did Beth mean when she said you were dating someone they all liked?" Gracie asked.

"It means you're very likable."

He totally avoided her question, but she was too curious to let him get away with it. "Who didn't your family like?"

Sebastian sighed and shook his head. "I guess they didn't think Rhonda Pearson and I were a good match."

"But you dated her for two years," she blurted.

His eyes widened, surprised by her knowledge apparently. "How do you know that?"

"Well, it wasn't exactly a secret. You and Rhonda made the Royal news a lot." Some of the entertainment pieces were positive, but there were other articles about them that didn't paint a rosy picture of the pair. And when Rhonda walked away from the relationship, she'd laid all the blame at his feet.

"Don't believe everything you read," he quipped.

"I try not to."

He nodded. "We had our up and downs, Rhonda and I."

"I hear she's back in town." Darn, her curiosity was getting the better of her.

Sebastian looked her square in the eye. "Is she? I wouldn't know."

"Must be hard. I mean, she broke your heart."

Sebastian made a face. "It's old news, Gracie. Let's not go there. It's my sister's wedding day and it's a happy occasion for my family."

Gracie cringed, wanting to take the conversation back. He was right. This was a happy day and she shouldn't let her insecurities about Sebastian get in the way of that. "Of course. I'm sorry." She took his hand, entwining their fingers, feeling the powerful connection. "Aren't you giving the toast soon?"

He glanced at their hands, looking pleased. "I am. Very soon."

"I can't wait to hear it."

He nuzzled her ear and brushed his lips to her throat. Something stirred in Gracie's heart. Desire, yes, they had that down pat. But it was more. The beginnings of...trust.

A short time later, Sebastian, being the eldest brother by three minutes, left the table they shared with Piper and Brian Cooper to toast the bride and groom. He sang Cam and Beth's praises, telling a few funny stories about Beth in her youth, amusing the guests. He was as charming as he was gracious and loving in his devotion to his sister. "Everyone, please raise your glass for Beth and Cam. May their lives be forever touched with happiness."

"Hear! Hear!" many of the guests chanted.

It was a beautiful moment, and Gracie, too, clinked glasses with Piper and Brian and then sipped her sparkling water.

"My nephew always knows the right thing to say." Piper's eyes beamed as Sebastian made his way back to the table. "I loved your toast," she told him.

"Yes, it was perfect," Gracie said.

Sebastian took his seat next to her again and thanked everyone. It was a little odd sitting with Brian and Sebastian's aunt Piper, Brian being Keith Cooper's nephew and all. But Brian had a hand in bringing his uncle's treachery to light, and had proven himself to be true-blue to the Wingate family. So much so he'd fallen in love with Piper, a woman eleven years his senior, and now they were a solid couple.

Gracie noticed Piper wasn't drinking champagne, either. She'd opted for sparkling water, as well. Every once in a while, Piper would put her hand on her tummy and make a face. Gracie knew that look.

Piper glanced at Brian, looking a little tentative. "I'm just a little bit…"

"It's okay." Brian took her hand and the love shining between them was truly beautiful. "We can tell them."

Piper smiled softly. "We didn't want to steal any of Beth's thunder today. We'd planned on telling the family later on, after the wedding…but I think it's okay to tell you. We're pregnant. Brian and I are having a baby."

Something flickered in Sebastian's eyes for a moment, before he caught himself and smiled. "Well, this is…" He searched for words.

"It's wonderful," Gracie filled in for him. "Congratulations, this is really great news."

"Yeah, congratulations, you two." Sebastian shook Brian's hand and leaned over to kiss his aunt's cheek. Piper was the cool, younger-minded aunt, from what Gracie could gather.

"I wasn't even sure I could have a child, but it appears sometimes miracles happen."

Brian kissed Piper's cheek. "*You're* the miracle," he said.

Gracie sensed Sebastian's eyes boring a hole in her back. They had news, too, but it would have to hold.

"I don't think Beth and Cam would mind hearing your news tonight," Sebastian said graciously.

"No." Brian shook his head. "Cam and Beth should have their day. We can wait to tell the rest of the family."

"I agree," Piper said. "I'm still getting used to the idea myself."

Gracie knew the feeling. No one had mentioned her pregnancy tonight, but she noticed inquisitive eyes watching her at times. His family was too discreet to confront her and ask questions, but what other conclusion could they come to, seeing her with Sebastian? It wasn't as if they'd ever shown interest in each other before this. And to be honest, it wasn't exactly Sebastian's style to date a pregnant woman. So yes, she supposed them being together today was cause for speculation.

It was what she'd been afraid of, what she'd suspected would happen.

"Your secret is safe with us," Sebastian told Piper, glancing at Gracie.

"That's right. Our lips are sealed." Gracie zipped her fingers over her mouth.

"Thank you both," Piper said.

The three-piece orchestra took their places again, and soon music filled the barn.

"That's my cue," Brian said, rising up and taking Piper's hand. "Are you up for a dance?"

"Of course."

The two took off to the dance floor, and Sebastian rose, as well. He didn't say a word, simply put out his hand. Gracie accepted it, and they, too, walked onto the dance floor. Under soft chandelier lighting, Sebastian spun her around slowly, holding her close, keeping their bodies connected. In his arms, the complications of her life fell away and everything seemed simple and easy. There was no need for words.

The rest of the night flew by in a blur. Gracie enjoyed the dinner, the dessert and more dancing with Sebastian. And finally, once the lovely wedding reception was over, Sebastian stood on her doorstep with no uncertainty that he would be coming inside.

Gracie took him by the hand and led him up the stairs and into her bedroom, both shedding their clothing along the way.

"I love waking up with you," Sebastian whispered, taking Gracie's hand and kissing each one of her knuckles. Dawn light streamed into her window, and she remembered falling asleep naked in Sebastian's arms after quite an exciting night.

"Mmm."

"I can't seem to get enough of you," he whispered. But the cliché didn't bother her, because she shared that sentiment. Slowly but surely, her walls of fear were crumbling. She was willing to open up more, to put aside her doubts and begin to believe.

"I feel the same way," she murmured.

"You do?" He touched a hand to her thigh and began stroking. Instantly her body reacted.

"Oh…yeah."

She was spooned next to him. Her heart pounded against her chest, her insides turned to mush and every part of her she'd thought was sated was now calling out for him, craving him again.

"Gracie, is this even possible?" he asked in total awe.

"Feels like it is," she said, only half teasing.

He cupped her head and kissed her flush on the lips, hard, demanding, claiming her as his own. At least in the moment, as she went willingly, loving the taste of him as he brushed their tongues, the scent of him as she breathed him in, loving the power of him as he held her hands above her head. He made love to her with his mouth and his hands, caressing her breasts, stroking her until she could barely take any more and then dipping down to please her below the waist.

She whimpered at his touch, the way he knew exactly what drove her wild, and when he brought her to completion, he kissed her again, riding the wave with her. And then he entered her, his power tempered by her body's limits, thrusting until he couldn't take it another second. He moved with grace and potency, and all the time giving to her as much as she was giving to him.

She came down to earth along with him, both of them breathless. "Gracie." He whispered her name like a solemn oath and hugged her to his chest. "Where do we go from here?"

Wasn't that her line? Except that she was too afraid to ask, too afraid to answer. "Now I make you the best breakfast you've ever had in your life."

She broke contact and moved quickly, tossing on clothes. She was running from her emotions, and Sebastian seemed to be struggling with his patience. He wanted to lay claim to his child, just as Piper and Brian had done last night, and she was the big mean culprit holding them back. At least that was how she felt. "Breakfast will be ready in thirty."

Sebastian clunked his head against the bed frame, defeat in his eyes. "You don't have to feed me."

"I want to. And you'll be glad I did."

"I'm sure. I'm glad of most of the things you do for me."

Gracie flushed at his deep rasp, the sexy way he was looking at her. He rose from bed, stark naked. Her eyes were riveted to his ripped chest, his narrow waist. A man couldn't be more beautiful. "I'll help."

She swallowed and lifted her eyes to his. "Okay."

She turned around and headed to the kitchen. Then

heard him rummaging through his clothes, his footsteps just seconds behind her.

"Have you ever had my mama's chorizo?"

His brows gathered. "No, how would I?"

"I thought maybe my papa would've brought some to your family once." She shrugged. "I guess not." She shoved a coffeepot into his hands. "Make coffee, please. I'll do the rest."

Gracie put a little butter and oil in a big cast-iron skillet, heated it up and added the chorizo, a mildly spicy variety, perfect for breakfast. Next, she tossed in day-old potatoes, cut into tiny chunks, and a cup of cooked black beans.

With the coffee brewing, she turned to Sebastian, who was sitting at the table watching her work at the stove. "It's important," she told Sebastian, "not to make a mush of this. We push the potatoes down carefully and try to fold everything together. Every family makes their own version of chorizo, with different spices and ingredients, and this is my mama's recipe." The scents rose up in a rush of steam, and she helped them along with waves of her hand. "Oh, smell that. It brings back such good memories for me."

She smiled at him. He was being sweet and she couldn't deny the incredible twenty-four hours they'd had together. "I wish I had time to make homemade tortillas. It's best with chorizo."

"Another time, maybe?"

"Yes, maybe."

A few minutes later, they took their seats and Gracie

served up the meal. Sebastian gobbled up every bite. The baby craved chorizo, too, and Gracie made quite a dent in her big dish. "So good."

His gaze lowered to her plate. "I like that you eat, Gracie."

"Most people do." He was too easy to tease.

"Not all women do."

"And you know *all* women?" she murmured.

"No. But…"

"Ah, most supermodels don't eat. Is that what you meant to say?"

"I take the Fifth." He put up his hand.

Funny he should compare her to his ex-girlfriend, right after the night they'd shared.

"It's really delicious, Gracie. Thank you for making it."

"I'm glad you—"

"What are you doing tonight?" he rushed out.

She shrugged. "I don't know, other than going by The Eatery and putting in a day's work."

"Have dinner with me. I want to take you someplace nice."

In her heart of hearts, she wanted to go. She wanted to spend more time with Sebastian, but it was all happening so fast. She was spinning, and she needed to stop and get off the ride for a little while. To regroup and think. Funny how, as a teen, she'd dreamed of being swept off her feet by Sebastian, and now that it was really happening, she had to slow it down. He was using a full-court press, which at any other time or situation she'd welcome. But not now. She didn't want to be rushed. She didn't want to make a mistake. Her baby and her future were at stake, and having great sex with Sebastian was only muddying the waters. She couldn't think clearly after being with him.

"I can't tonight."

The light in his green eyes dimmed. "Why not?"

"I need…some time."

He sighed loud enough to make her shudder. His patience was running thin. "Then when?"

"Tomorrow night?"

"Fine. I'll pick you up at seven."

He walked out of the room then, without another word.

# Seven

The next day, Sebastian searched the grounds of the Royal park, his eyes honing in on every person he spotted. There were joggers and people walking their dogs at a brisk pace. He also spotted two toddlers bundled up in bright blue bibbed jackets on the swings, their mother's pushes sending them flying as their squeals of laughter rang out. A lone gray-haired man sat on a bench, his arms crossed to ward off the cold.

Sebastian looked at the text message Rhonda had sent earlier today. He's playing football with his friends at the park after school.

"No, he's not," he murmured. Lonny wasn't here. There were no football players at the park. Sebastian had been here watching and waiting for the better part of an hour. He'd offered to help the boy and he thought it best to make it a chance encounter, but Lonny was a no-show. Sighing, he eyed the park perimeter one last time, making sure he hadn't missed anything. Still no sign of Lonny. He headed to the parking lot. Rhonda was there, leaning against his car, waiting for him.

"Rhonda? What are you doing here?"

Distress marred her perfect face and tears ran down her cheeks. "Lonny ditched school today, and we had a big fight and he stormed out. I can't find him anywhere. I thought maybe he'd be here. You know, with his friends. I had to come check for myself."

"I haven't seen him, Rhonda. I've been here awhile."

She broke down entirely then, her tears turning into big, heaving sobs. "I'm…sorry to involve you in this. I just don't know what to do…"

"It's okay, Rhonda. He's a little mixed up right now, but he's not a bad kid."

"I feel…like it's…all my fault." She hung her head down and Sebastian drew her into his arms. She needed a hug right now, and some compassion.

"It's not your fault, Rhonda. He's a headstrong kid. He'll come around."

Sebastian believed that. Having been orphaned at a young age, Lonny was acting out right now, a form of rebellion at his lot in life. It wasn't easy having a supermodel sister, someone known around the world for her swimsuit layouts. "Tell you what? Let's go for a drive and try to find him together. You know where his friends live?"

She nodded. "Most of them."

"We'll start there."

"Really? You'd do that?" She smiled through her tears.

"Yes. Come on. I bet we find him before the sun goes down." Which was in just two hours, so they really had to move. "Okay?"

Rhonda cupped his face in her hands and kissed him briefly on the lips, her eyes shining with gratitude. "Thank you."

He opened the car door for her. "Get in. We're burnin' daylight."

Rhonda chuckled at his attempt at humor and got into his car. The truth was, he was worried about the kid, too. Boys at that age were reckless, at times. He and Sutton surely had been and they'd gotten into trouble more than once, but nothing like what Lonny was going through. One wrong move could change Lonny's whole life forever.

"The family's buzzing about you dating Sebastian," Sutton said, handing Gracie a cup of Lauren's special hot cocoa, a teasing smile on his handsome face. He had many of the same expressions as his twin, and sometimes it was like a sense of déjà vu being with him.

"Thanks." She warmed her hands up around the mug. They sat at a back table at The Eatery. It was their slow time, the hours between lunch and dinner, when they could all take a breather. "Buzzing how?"

Lauren tugged on her ponytail. "What do you think?

They've known you and your family for years. Everyone's thrilled."

"Are they?"

Gracie was a pretty confident woman, but when it came to her place in the Wingate empire, she had her doubts. She certainly hadn't thought she'd be so welcome. Or was it the lottery win that had her in their good graces now?

"You're like family already," Sutton said.

Gracie eyed him, raising her brow.

He got the hint. "Sebastian's been happier lately."

Gracie liked hearing that from Sebastian's twin. The two brothers were incredibly close, and it was as if she was hearing it from Sebastian himself. Although they hadn't parted too happily last evening. Sebastian was losing patience with her.

"So what's on your agenda tonight?" Lauren asked. "Got a hot date with my future brother-in-law or anything?"

"Actually, I do. Soon as I finish up here, I'm going home to change."

"Where's he taking you?" her partner asked.

"I have no idea. He wouldn't say. Other than it's someplace special."

"Special is always good."

Gracie's cell phone rang and she noted the number. "Excuse me. I've got to get this," she told Lauren and Sutton. Then she walked into the office and closed the door.

"Hello, yes, this is Gracie Diaz. Thanks for calling me back."

"No problem, Ms. Diaz. This is Trudy Metcalf from the Royal Birthing Center. I understand you're interested in taking early bird classes. Congratulations, by the way, on your pregnancy."

"Thank you. Yes, I think it's about time I sign up. Although I've been reading everything I can get my hands on about having a baby."

"It's all good. How far along are you?"

"I'm about fourteen weeks now, and I'm in very good health."

"Great, we want to keep it that way. That's what our early bird classes are all about."

Gracie spent a few more minutes on the phone with Trudy, signing up for classes. Once the call was over, it was as if another step in her life's plan was finally coming together. Never mind the morning sickness or the fuller waist or the huge appetite now, signing up for childbirth classes made her pregnancy and the new life she would bring into this world a beautiful reality.

Gracie left The Eatery at five in the afternoon to get ready for her date with Sebastian. She was grateful for Sutton's and Lauren's support. It meant a lot to her and made her feel a tad bit better about dating Sebastian. She strode into her rental home, proceeded upstairs, stripped off her clothes and stepped into a hot shower. Warmth immediately seeped into her bones, easing her tension with the help of a freshly scented lavender scrub.

After the shower, she took her time drying off, looking at the mirror to examine the subtle changes in her waist. It was a good thing and meant her baby was thriving. "Can't wait to meet you, little one," she murmured.

Gracie rummaged through her closet, looking for just the right dress for her date. Sebastian said he was taking her someplace special, and she wanted to look the part. She pulled out one dress after another, making a small mound on her bed until she hit upon just the right one. It was a creamy taupe with a plunging neckline, blending well with her skin tones, its folds draping a little past the knee. Was it too much? She'd never worn it before. But her decision was made as soon as she tried it on. The fit was perfect, and she wasn't going to be shy around Sebastian.

She fastened a thin gold choker around her neck and added hoop earrings. The look warranted a special do with her hair, so she fussed with it, coming up with a messy uplift that appeared salon-worthy.

With a few minutes to spare, Gracie sat down in the living room and called her mother. She liked to check in with her several times a week. And loved that she could now afford to give her mom and brother a good life in Florida. It meant the world to her. "Hello, Mama. It's me."

"Gracie, my heart, it's good to hear your voice. It's been a few days."

"*Si*, Mama. But just a few. How are you and our little Enrico today?"

"Our little Enrico is getting taller than your mama," she said. "He's well. He's out with friends right now.

Nice boys. But how about you, Graciella? How is the baby?"

Her mother never could understand her need to have a baby on her own. Alisa Diaz was too traditional to think of conceiving a child any other way. And Gracie finally had confided in her mama the situation with Sebastian. Not the details, goodness no, but at least now she did know know the truth about the baby's father. And her mother was being supportive.

"We're both fine. I am feeling well, Mama. I signed up for childbirth classes."

"That's good. And Sebastian? Will he be going with you?"

"He's… I'm not sure, Mama. But we're going out on a date tonight."

"It is working out, then?"

It was hard for her mother not to push. And she understood that. Alisa simply wanted to see her daughter settled and happy. "*Si*, Mama, but we are going slow."

"How slow? You are already pregnant!"

Gracie chuckled. Her mother had a way of putting things in perspective. "You know what I mean. I want… I want what you and Papa had."

"Ah, I see." Her mother paused and then added, "So your plans have not changed? You won't be coming to Florida to live with us?"

"No, Mama, I won't. Right now, my life is here. My new estate has plenty of room for when you come to visit."

It was past seven when she ended the call. Actually,

it was half an hour past, and Gracie looked at her texts to see if Sebastian had been delayed. Nothing yet.

Five minutes later, she was just about to send him a text when his message came through. I'm sorry. Something came up last minute and I have to cancel. I promise to make it up to you.

Gracie stared at the message a long time. It sounded rushed and impersonal and cold.

She texted him back. Are you okay?

She didn't receive an answer until an hour later, when he simply wrote, I'm fine.

Gracie had never been stood up before, and it hit her right in the gut. She was disappointed, for sure, and curious as to what had happened tonight to keep Sebastian from calling her beforehand. From giving her a better explanation. "All dressed up and nowhere to go, Gracie," she murmured. She kicked off her shoes, changed out of her clothes and threw on a pair of comfortable gray sweats. The night she thought was just beginning had come to a grinding and discouraging halt.

In the morning, Gracie stopped by the Texas Cattleman's Club. It was a prestigious club, generations old, that catered to rich and powerful businessmen, and now businesswomen, who lived in the vicinity and had a valued stake in Texas commerce.

Austere, with dark wood walls and furnishings, the club had gone through a bit of transformation lately. It had become more female-friendly, with brighter interiors and updated facilities. Although the old private rooms still existed, the tone of the club had totally changed. But what remained was the rule that one had to be a member or a member's guest to use the facilities. Thank goodness for Beth. She'd invited her countless times to play tennis here, to go to the day spa with her and to use the pool. But now it was her turn to become a full-fledged member, and she was especially interested in the recently updated day care center for the baby.

The receptionist at the desk recognized her. Being Royal's only mega lottery winner had some advantages. "You're Gracie Diaz."

"Yes, that's me."

"It's very nice to meet you. What can I do for you today, Ms. Diaz?"

"Well, for one, I'd like to apply to become a member of the club. I know it takes a vote, but I want to get the process started. If that's okay?"

"Yes, I think that's fine. You do know you need to be recommended, right?"

"Yes, I don't think that should be a problem." Or *would* it? She didn't come from old money. In fact, her money was as new as it could get. But those archaic notions were just that, and she was pretty sure that when Beth and Cam got back from their honeymoon, they would help her. Sebastian could, too, but she didn't want to ask him.

She was still a bit put off about being stood up last night. He'd never called. And she didn't know what to make of that.

The receptionist handed her a form to fill out and she thanked her.

"I was wondering if I could take a peek at the day care center?"

"Why, um, sure." The woman took off her glasses and set them on her desk. "I could probably take a minute to show you."

"That's great, thank you."

Boisterous laughter making its way from the hallway interrupted her thoughts. She turned and found Sebastian walking alongside a gray-haired man. The two were oblivious to anyone else, Sebastian's smile wide. Apparently, whatever crisis he'd had last night, *when he'd stood her up*, was over and done with. He looked like he didn't have a care in the world.

Then suddenly, their eyes met. And she had to give him credit—he didn't flinch or look away when he spotted her. Instead, he bade the man farewell and headed over to her. "Gracie," he said, "what are you doing here?"

"I'm…checking out the day care center among other things."

The receptionist rose from her desk. "I was just going to show her the room, Mr. Wingate."

Sebastian's eyes lit up. "I can do that. I know where it is. I can take her."

The receptionist exchanged glances with both of them, unsure, and then the phone rang. "Excuse me, I have to get this," she said.

"We'll just be going," he told her and the woman nodded as she took the call.

Sebastian took Gracie's elbow and they walked down a corridor. "I'm so sorry about last night, Gracie. I really missed seeing you."

She stopped in her tracks. "Did you?"

"I did."

"I don't understand why you couldn't call, instead of leaving me hanging."

Sebastian looked away and hesitated. "It's a long story, Gracie." His gaze traveled the length of the hallway, a note of caution in his eyes. "I'll share it with you, but this isn't the place, Gracie. Trust me on this."

He took her hand, entwining their fingers, and the connection warmed her heart. How could one man elicit so many emotions in her? Desire, doubt, anger, joy. They were all there, simmering under the surface. "Come on, let's go check out the day care center. I promise to explain everything to you when I can."

She frowned, but he kept looking at her with those deep green eyes, penetrating her good sense, giving her hope that he had a valid explanation that would clear up her misgivings.

"Okay," she said.

"Great." He flashed her a big smile.

A minute later, they were awash in the bright colors of the day care center, blues and greens, pinks and yellows and oranges.

"Would you look at this?" Sebastian seemed to be in awe. There were five children in the center. Two little girls playing dress-up, yanking out princess costumes from a treasure chest. Three boys were on alphabet mats, messing around with miniature cars. The room was large, and there was a painting station, a reading circle and a polished wood playhouse complete with a second story for the children to frolic on.

"I'm looking," she said, taking it all in, as well.

The woman in charge walked over to them. "Hello, how can I help you?"

"We're just here to observe," Sebastian said. "For the future."

"Well, as long as you're a member, you're welcome to do that anytime. My name is Katherine. Please let me know if you have any questions."

"Of course. Thank you," Gracie said. When the day care worker walked back to the children, she put her hand on her tummy. "It's hard to believe I'll have a little one like this soon."

"*We'll* have," he corrected. "And I'm with you. It's still hard to take in."

"My mama says every baby is a little prize from God," she whispered.

Sebastian gave her hand a squeeze. "I think your mama is right."

She smiled then, and her anger ebbed. Sebastian asked for her trust. It wasn't easy to give, but for the sake of their baby, she had to try.

She had questions for the day care teacher, but they could wait. It was enough to see the place and envision her child here one day, once she became a full-fledged member of TCC. "I should go. I have other appointments."

She began walking toward the exit with Sebastian at her side. Once they reached the parking lot, he took both of her hands in his and gazed down at her. "I have a busy day, too, but I'd like to see you tonight."

She shook her head. "I'm sorry. I'm busy."

"Doing?"

"For a man who likes to keep secrets, you're awfully nosy."

"Gracie."

"Teasing, Sebastian. I'm going to meet with Tom Riley, my Realtor, later on. I'm looking for a little office space of my own."

"Is it like a date?"

Her eyes rolled. "Married, three children."

"Teasing, Gracie."

"Funny, Sebastian." She had to keep on her toes around him. He wasn't slow on the uptake at all.

"So you need office space?"

She nodded. "Yeah, I do, or I will at some point in the future." She had every intention of starting her own event-planning business. It was something she was good at and loved doing. Now that she had the means, nothing was stopping her from looking into it.

Something flickered in Sebastian's eyes at the mention of her future, but he snapped out of it pretty quickly. "How about I come over after? I owe you and want to make up for being a no-show last night."

He caught her in a weak moment and she had a pretty good idea how he was going to make it up to her. The thought sizzled in her mind and made her insides swirl with heat. "Maybe."

He chuckled. "Only *maybe*? I must be losing my touch."

"Believe me, you're not." His touch was just fine. More than just fine. And he proved it by lifting her chin with his knuckles and planting a delicious kiss on her lips.

He gazed at her then, his eyes gleaming with promise. It was really hard to concentrate after a Sebastian kiss. "Good to know," he said. "I'll call you tonight."

Sebastian rode up the elevator to the sixth floor of Wingate Enterprises, which was just outside Royal proper, and entered his executive office. He had a lot on his mind, so he really didn't see Sutton initially, not until he gazed up and found his twin at the bar pouring bourbon into two tumblers.

"Hey, what's up?" he said, removing his jacket.

"Not much, just crisis number twelve."

"Only twelve? Seems like we've weathered more storms than that lately."

Sutton set the tumbler on his desk while he sipped his own drink. "Seems that way, doesn't it? Drink up."

Sebastian gathered his brows. "Force-feeding me alcohol. This must be bad." He sipped bourbon and it warmed his throat going down.

"Not horrible, but not great, either. It seems WinJet is doing fine, and since we've concentrated on the new branding of our hotels, we're solid there. But we're still in need of some good investments to keep our other US holdings afloat."

"Okay," he said, thinking about the ramifications of that. "So we'll find some capital. Somehow."

"How? We're already maxed out. Since the scandal hit the papers, many of our investors are already on edge. They're not going to want to increase their risk any more than they have to."

Sebastian began nodding. "I get that. So what'll we do? Sell?"

"I don't want to do that. We'll lose a fortune, and honestly, some of those smaller companies are worth the trouble. They were Dad's vision and have been with us from the beginning. Jobs are at stake and people's livelihoods."

"I don't want to sell, either." Sebastian took another swig of bourbon. "Maybe we should talk to Mom about this?"

"And go into the belly of the beast?"

Sebastian laughed. "Okay, not my brightest idea. Give me a few days. I'll think of something."

"You got it." Sutton eyed his brother carefully. "So I hear Gracie's going to childbirth classes. You must be excited about that."

Sebastian set his glass down and stared at his brother. "Childbirth classes? This is the first I'm hearing about it."

"Uh-oh. Me and my big mouth. Lauren's going to punch my lights out for this."

"Lauren knows? Am I the last person to find this

out?" A knot twisted in his gut. Why didn't Gracie tell him about this? He had every right to know about the classes.

"Sorry, bro. I didn't realize…"

"Not your fault. Gracie still has issues with me. She's being cautious and I get it." He picked up his bourbon and took a swallow. "Actually, I *don't* get it. We're having a baby together. I need to be there. And I don't have a clue why she wants to go this alone."

"Give it time. I mean it wasn't as if you two went about this in the conventional way. You didn't show an interest in her until you learned about the baby. That would put any woman on edge. You have to build up her trust."

"Trust? Okay. I'm rusty at all this. Haven't had a woman in my life since Rhonda."

Sutton eyed him cautiously. "I hear she's back in town."

"Yeah, she is."

Last night, Sebastian and Rhonda had searched high and low for her brother, Lonny. They'd finally found the kid, along with three other delinquent boys, a rowdy crowd if he ever saw one, just outside town.

They'd obviously been up to no good. Lonny took one look at him, and had nearly caved on the spot. Sebastian had calmed the boy down and had a heart-to-heart talk with him. Lonny had confessed to vandalizing an abandoned house, breaking windows, destroying what was left of the furniture. Sebastian had told him he had to report what he'd done to the local police. The kid had been scared, but he'd followed through, with Sebastian and Rhonda right by his side.

Luckily, Sebastian had been able to pull some strings with Judge Haymore, his TCC buddy, the one he'd been speaking to when he spotted Gracie this morning, and the police had let Lonny go with a stern warning, after extracting a promise from him to clean up the mess he'd made. It was good Sebastian had reconnected with Lonny last night, and he hoped like hell he'd gotten through to the boy.

"You guess so? Have you seen her?"

He nodded. "I have. It's not what you think."

"Good, because what I'm thinking…"

"Don't. There's nothing between Rhonda and me but friendship."

"Try to keep it that way." Sutton slapped him on the back. But already his mind had returned to Gracie, and how he could, for lack of a better term, get back in her good graces.

# Eight

It ended up being an early evening after all. Tom, her Realtor, had limited spaces to show her, the inventory being low right now. And none of the three places he'd shown her would work. One was too far outside town, another was so small it gave her claustrophobia and the last one was frankly almost on top of Wingate Enterprises. Like right across the street. No can do. But at least she got an idea of what was out there.

Gracie changed into a pair of cozy pajamas, made herself a bowl of soup and put her feet up on the sofa. It was quiet in the house, and at eight thirty, it was too early to go to sleep. For the next thirty minutes, she channel-surfed her flat screen, unable to find anything on TV she wanted to watch. Gracie sighed. She was antsy and restless, which she couldn't figure out since she'd had a full day today. Her cell phone rang, and she rose from the sofa to answer it.

"Hello."

"Hi, it's me." The low drawl of Sebastian's voice made her heart skip a beat.

"Hello, you. I didn't think you'd call. It's late." Actually, it wasn't all that late, but she wasn't going to make this easy for him.

"I wanted to give you time to finish up with your Realtor. How'd it go?"

"Not too well, but I'm sure I'll find something."

"That's too bad. So what are you doing right now?"

"Right now, just relaxing, or at least trying to."

"Ready for bed?"

"Maybe."

"Before you go, can you open the front door?"

Her pulse began to pound. "Open the front door? Why?"

"You'll see."

She walked over to the window and peered out. Sebastian's car was parked in front of her house. Oh, God! What was he doing here? She was a total mess, covered in soft flannel, her hair in a ponytail, her makeup all washed off. Gracie really didn't want him to see her like this, but then, how could she send him away? She sighed, straightened out her pj's, finger-combed her hair and opened the door slowly. And came face-to-face with a big gray stuffed elephant. With pink ears. And then she noticed a bag filled with chocolate raspberry sticks.

Not the gourmet kind, and not in a fancy box, but her very favorite from the grocery store. There were flowers, too, a bouquet of at least two dozen roses in various shades of red, from crimson-tipped to bloodred. Behind all that was the man, his face hidden until he peeked out from behind the elephant. "Hi."

Gracie couldn't believe it. "What is all this?"

"An apology for last night. And if you're not up for company, that's okay. I'll just leave this all with you."

"For heaven's sake, Sebastian. Come inside." She ushered him inside the house and they stood looking at each other, his eyes gleaming.

"An elephant?" she asked.

"You have a collection of them, right?"

Oh, wow. How did he find all this out? He knew about her elephant obsession as a kid. He knew her favorite candy. The man had done his homework. "Right."

She took the elephant off his hands and admired it. It was plush and soft and cuddly. "Is this for the baby?"

"It's for you. The baby will have its own parade of animals."

And then there was silence, an awareness between them that sizzled as they stared at each other. Sebastian set the flowers and candy down. "I can go. But I don't want to."

She didn't want him to leave, either. "Stay."

He gave her a heart-stopping smile. "That's all I needed to hear."

Then he pulled her close, his lips claiming hers, hot and hungry and utterly delicious. One kiss became two and then three, and soon Sebastian had her back against the wall, cupping her face in his big, strong hands, making love to her mouth in a frenzy that stole her breath. She was awash with emotion, with crazy desire, and wanted to touch all of him. Wanted to feel his skin under her fingertips. She pulled at his jacket and then his shirt, unable to get to him fast enough between kisses.

He helped her tug off his shirt and toss it away. She stroked his bare chest, loving the feel of his power under her fingertips, loving the heat of his body, feeling his growing desire below his waist. He groaned in pleasure, telling her he loved what she was doing to him.

It was easy for him to find her skin, his hands slipping under her pajama top, pushing up the material, cupping her breasts and thumbing the hardened peaks. "Oh, man," he whispered in her ear. "You're perfect."

It was all too fevered and crazed, as if time was running out, as if they were in some sort of passionate race. Sebastian's kisses made her dizzy, her body pliant in his arms. And so when he slipped his hand along her tummy and then dipped below her navel, separating her pajama pants from her skin, she opened her mouth at the pleasure and moaned his name. "Sebastian."

"I know, sweetheart," he whispered, his fingertips touching her very core. She moaned again and again as he stroked her there, while kissing her lips, touching their tongues. Her release came quickly, hard, loud and fast as she cried out, the immense pleasure splintering her into a thousand pieces.

It was hot and heavy and so very, very good. She was

in deep now. Her hard, outer shell cracking, melting, crumbling. She wasn't sure that was enough. But a man who could make her wild like this, who sparked emotions in her that no one ever had, a man who seemed to know her inside and out, was a difficult one to turn away. She was afraid she was falling in love with him.

Sebastian lifted her into his powerful arms and carried her to the bedroom. He knew the way now, and there was comfort in that, that maybe he belonged right where he was. Then he lowered her onto the bed, and she wasn't shy about removing her clothes, then removing what remained of his.

He was beautiful to look at, especially in his aroused state, tall and tanned and broad-shouldered. And his end-of-the-day facial scruff only made him look more devastatingly handsome.

"Gracie," he said, coming over her. "There's never been anyone like you before."

She smiled, her heart warm, filled with love. "I feel the same way."

His eyes beamed bright, right before he joined their bodies. She cooed at the familiar, welcome feel of him and he sighed, as if…he was coming home.

Sebastian lay on Gracie's bed, watching the beauty beside him sleep. She had been resistant, until tonight. Something seemed to have changed in her. He noticed her giving a little bit more, opening up to the possibility of the two of them. Maybe she was starting to trust in him, trust in *them* as a couple?

Hell, it was all confusing. But he wanted what they were experiencing to continue. He wanted their relationship to grow. Yet, at the same time, he wasn't going to overthink this. Too much was at stake. As hard as it was, he was going to try to let things evolve naturally. Gracie couldn't be pushed. He didn't want her to shy away or run scared.

He stroked her head, pushing aside a few stray strands of hair as she slept. It was dawn now, the light streaming into the room, telling him the world was waking up. So was he. He rose from the bed quietly and looked at the time. It was just after 6:00 a.m. and it was time for a shower and a cup of coffee.

Sebastian showered first, dressing again in yesterday's clothes. He'd have to stop by home and pick up a change of clothes. And then a thought struck. How nice would it be to move in with Gracie, have his stuff here, so that they could be together every day?

He scoffed at the notion. She would never go for that. They weren't there yet, but maybe one day they would be. Maybe one day she'd trust him enough to tell him about the classes she'd signed up for. It really bugged him that she'd shut him out of that part of her life so far.

In the kitchen, Sebastian made coffee, and as it brewed, he scavenged around to find something to make for breakfast. He wasn't a great cook, but he could scramble eggs and fry up some bacon. She had turkey bacon, a healthier alternative to the real thing. He got those things started and then poured two glasses of orange juice.

Gracie stumbled into the room, looking groggy, her

hair disheveled and her pajama top wrinkled. He had never seen anything more adorable. "Mornin', sweetheart."

She smiled and walked straight into his arms. It was such a pleasant surprise he didn't know what to do with his hands at first, but then he gently wrapped them around her.

"Good morning to you, too." Gracie laid her head on his chest, snuggling into him, and a delicious warmth traveled through his body.

"How did Sleeping Beauty sleep last night?"

She choked back a laugh. "I'm no beauty. I'm a mess."

He hugged her tighter. "Not from where I'm standing. You look cute."

She groaned. "Ugh."

"I'm making breakfast," he announced. As if she couldn't tell by the pungent smell of bacon cooking and coffee brewing. "Are you hungry?"

She turned her face up to gaze into his eyes. "A little. I need a shower first."

"Go, I'll finish up in here. And then I'll serve you."

"You really don't have to do that. But thanks." She broke from their embrace and turned to leave.

"Hey?" he called to her. "You okay?"

She faced him, gathering her brows as if he'd asked a silly question. "I'm...perfect. You said so yourself last night."

"I meant every word."

"Yeah," she said with a tilt of her head. "I think you did."

She left the room with a whimsical smile on her face and Sebastian felt a stirring deep in his belly. It was a good feeling, like the moment he'd spot his presents under the tree on Christmas morning. Suddenly, he could imagine a lifetime of waking up next to Gracie. He welcomed the thought and wondered if they'd ever get there.

"I feel human again," Gracie said a short time later, returning to the kitchen dressed in a tailored pair of slacks and a deep rose sweater. Her hair was still a little wet, the dark locks in a natural part to the side. Her complexion was flawless, her skin smooth. Pregnancy had bloomed on her and he could only smile at her.

"Human and all woman," he replied with a wink. "Come sit down. Breakfast is ready."

"So you're really serving me?" She took a seat.

"Of course. But don't judge me too harshly, sweetheart. I'm not a great cook."

"Because you never had to cook for yourself. You always had someone do it for you."

She said it good-naturedly and he didn't take offense. "I did, up until recently, when my world crashed around me. Hey, I'm not playing the victim here, just so you know. I'm grateful for everything I've ever had in my life."

"Humble, I like that."

"I think you like *me*, too, a little."

She picked up her orange juice and took a sip. "Maybe."

"I just get a maybe? I thought after last night, I'd be a little higher up the scale than that."

She blushed, a full rosy color reaching her cheeks. "Well, the elephant was a nice touch."

Sebastian let out a chuckle. Damn, it was hard getting her to give an inch verbally, but he still thought they were making great progress in the bedroom. What they had there was scalding hot and delicious and that meant something staggering. "Let's eat."

She put her head down to gaze at her food. "And yes, if you must know, I like you, a little." Then she picked up her fork triumphantly and dug into the meal.

Sebastian only shook his head at her.

A week later, Gracie walked into The Eatery during the six o'clock dinner hour and made her way into the kitchen. She'd spent the better part of the afternoon with Tom Riley searching for the right office space for her event business and so far, she wasn't having any luck finding the right space in the right location.

Lauren was at the workstation, overseeing the dishes being brought out for the customers. She glanced over her shoulder and they made eye contact. "Hey, what are you doing here? Thought you had a hot date with Sebastian again. It's been like four nights in a row."

"Five, but who's counting," she said. "And we did have a date, but he canceled at the last minute."

"Oh, sorry to hear that. It happens sometimes." Lauren wiped her hands on a dish towel and walked over to her. "The Wingate twins are notorious for their work ethic. I bet something came up that he couldn't get out of."

"Maybe, but he's canceled twice this week, and I

wouldn't mind, but he's very cryptic about why he's canceling. And then apologizes like crazy."

Lauren walked over to her and gave her shoulders a squeeze. "It's not too busy right now and I'm ready for a break. Let's go into the lounge and have a bite to eat. I'd say let's go for drinks, but—" she gazed at Gracie's belly and winked "—that'll have to wait. C'mon, girlfriend, let's sit down and talk. There's a Tex-Mex pizza with our names on it. I'll bring it over."

And just a short time later, Gracie was biting into a piping hot pizza smothered with cheese and veggies, topped with Tabasco sauce and jalapeños. She looked across the table at Lauren. "Hmm, so good."

"It's getting to be a customer favorite." Lauren bit into her pizza and chewed. "This just might be marginally better than anything Sebastian had in store for you tonight."

Gracie nearly choked on her food and then managed, "Could be."

Lauren smiled, and then she took on a thoughtful expression. "You know, I think Sebastian has a lot on his mind. He and Sutton are worried about their cash flow. They have over a dozen companies that are struggling. It's not public knowledge, Gracie. Maybe that's what he's working on. Sebastian probably doesn't want to bore you with his problems. I mean, you two are on the honeymoon side of dating."

Gracie stared at her friend, her mind spinning. She thought the money the Wingates received from the sale of the house had put them over the top. "Are you saying Wingate Enterprises still needs money?"

Lauren nodded, lowering her voice. "Yes, except for the hotels and WinJet, Wingate Enterprises could use an influx of cash. At least, that's what Sutton tells me. And this is just between you and me."

She nodded. "Of course. Thanks for telling me. I won't say a word to anyone."

Gracie could keep a secret, but she only wished Sebastian had confided in her. Why hadn't he? Was it pride? She fought to put off the other places her mind was going.

*He needs money for his company.*

*I have money.*

Gracie didn't want to go here. She didn't want to think that Sebastian was using her to get his hands on her money.

"Hey," Lauren said, as if reading her mind. "Sebastian really cares about you. You have to know that by now. He's one of the good guys, Gracie."

Gracie smiled. She was starting to believe that. This past week, they'd had a great time together. The two of them were growing closer, and they were learning new things about each other every day. She wasn't thinking about the way they burned up the sheets, though that was off-the-charts good. It was more, and she saw it in Sebastian's eyes whenever he looked at her.

"I had my doubts about Sutton and that whole mess with the dating mix-up and Sebastian," Lauren confided. "I thought Sutton was tricking me and lying to me…and it was all so confusing. But when it's meant to be, it finally comes together. I sense that with you and Sebastian. Even if you don't see it yet."

"Maybe I'm beginning to."

"Then trust what you're feeling, Gracie. Open up your heart. Let him in."

The thought of opening her heart to Sebastian wasn't novel. Heavens, she'd dreamed of him for years, and now all of her fantasies were coming true. He was the man she'd been attracted to at the masquerade ball. And the father of her child, the man who'd earned her trust. Perhaps it was time to finally accept that. Maybe, against all odds, she was meant to love and be loved by Sebastian. "Thank you, Lauren. I always feel better after I talk to you."

"That's what friends are for."

She was grateful for Lauren's friendship. She reached over to take the other woman's hand. "I'm glad we're friends."

Lauren nodded. "Me, too. I mean, who knows, maybe one day we'll be more than friends. I mean, it'll be cool if all the stars align, and you and I become family. As in sisters-in-law."

And she was amazed Lauren's notion didn't send her into an immediate tizzy.

It felt sort of…right.

The next day, Gracie made an unannounced visit to Sebastian's office. She had a song in her heart as she rode the elevator to the sixth floor of the building and got off. The receptionist greeted her from behind her half-moon-shaped glass desk. "Hello, how can I help you?" the woman asked.

Behind her, the Wingate Enterprises sign, carved out of teak, shone with a glowing polish. Everything in this building spoke of contemporary design and success.

"I'm here to see Sebastian Wingate."

The woman looked at her computer. "Do you have an appointment?"

"No, but if you tell him that Gracie Diaz is here to see him, he might find time."

The woman smiled. "I will do that." She buzzed in, and announced just that.

She could hear Sebastian on the other end. "Please show her in, Lois."

"Right this way." The receptionist had only taken a few steps toward the wide double doors to her left when Sebastian flung them open and spotted her. "Gracie! This is a surprise."

"A good one, I hope." Lois put her head down and Sebastian grinned.

"Thanks, Lois. I'll take it from here. Hold my calls, please."

And then he reached for her hand and tugged. "Come in. Is everything all right?" He shut the doors behind them.

Gracie laughed. "Everything's fine."

"Okay, great." He nodded his head. "It's good to see you."

"It's good to see you, too." His eyes sparkled and she

had a good idea hers did, too, as they stared at each for a few long seconds.

Then instinct took over and Sebastian reached for her, just as she reached for him. And the kiss they shared was more than the meeting of their lips—it was a welcome, an invitation, a promise. Sebastian broke off the kiss but hugged her so tight she thought she'd burst from joy. "This made my day," he whispered in her ear. "Seeing you was just what I needed."

"Really? Are you having a bad day?"

"It's better now that you're here." He kissed her again and tenderly brushed a few locks of hair away from her face. The way he touched her, the way he looked at her, brought ribbons of warmth to her heart. Finally, in his arms, she felt safe and maybe a little bit loved.

Maybe Lauren was right, maybe Sebastian didn't want to burden her with his work problems, because he never really brought the subject up. "I didn't want to interrupt you if you were busy, but I took a chance at coming here."

"I'm glad you did."

She broke away from him to look around his office. "So this is where you spend a lot of your time."

"Some days, yes."

She peered out the window, and from the sixth story, she had a breathtaking view of blue skies above and the town of Royal below laid out before her. "Only some days? What do you do the other days?"

"Have meetings with bankers, and lawyers, and politicians."

Gracie made a face.

"I know, it's no fun. But sometimes, I get to see a beautiful woman, and it makes it all worth it."

Gracie spun around and stared into his eyes. "Really?"

"You have to know, seeing you is the best part of my day and…night."

She didn't know. But she was beginning to. And that made her heart open up wider, letting him in, loving him even more than she thought possible.

"I do have a reason for this visit."

"You do? You mean it wasn't just to put a happy face to my day?"

She smiled. "What are you doing on Saturday morning?"

He gave her a puzzled look and shook his head. "I don't know. Seeing you?"

"I need a partner for my early bird classes, and I—"

"Yes." He took the steps to bridge the gap between them quickly. "Yes. I'm your partner, Gracie. I wouldn't miss it."

He put a hand on her tummy, something he'd done many times before in the heat of passion. But this time was different; this caress meant more. She was finally putting her faith in him, letting go of her doubts and tearing down the walls that had kept her from trusting him.

"You have no idea how much this means to me. I want this, Gracie. I want more with you."

"I think I do know," she whispered back. "I want that, too."

Sebastian took her into his arms again and kissed her tenderly. "I can't wait for Saturday now."

"Neither can I."

Gracie sat cross-legged on a yoga mat in the Pregna-Gym at the birth center, Sebastian by her side, as the childbirth instructor introduced herself. "Hi, I'm Maddy, and first of all I want to say congratulations! This is an exciting time in your lives and I'm honored to be a part of it. We'll be together for the next four weeks, getting your mind and body ready to welcome your child into the world. Now, if we can go around the room and find out who you are and what brought you to this class…"

Several couples introduced themselves. When it was Gracie's turn, knowing eyes gazed at her and Sebastian, as if introductions were not necessary. She was the millionaire lottery winner in Royal, and he was one of the most eligible, recently scandalized, bachelors in Maverick County, a Wingate no less. "I'm Gracie, and I want to learn everything there is to know about having a healthy pregnancy and doing what's right for the baby. This is my coach, Sebastian."

Sebastian smiled to the group.

There were six couples in all sitting in the circle, and after the introductions were made, the instructor passed out a workbook and asked them to take a few minutes to look it over. Gracie shared the workbook with Sebastian, and quietly they turned the pages, heads together, seeing a whole new world opening up before them.

"This is surreal," Sebastian whispered. "In a good way."

"I know. Like, in less than six months, the baby will be here."

Sebastian laid his hand over her wrist and gave a squeeze. "Are you scared?"

"A little." Then she faced him. "I've been wanting a baby for so long, but I have to admit it is a bit daunting."

"I'll be with you every step of the way."

She nodded, grateful for his support, noticing wandering gazes landing on them from around the circle. "I think we've been recognized," she said under her breath.

"I think so, too. Are you okay with it?" he asked.

"I guess I have no choice now. But yes, I'm okay."

Sebastian's eyes flickered and his approval was written all over his face. He kissed her cheek, a sweet little kiss that packed quite a punch. "Me, too."

"Okay, class, now it's time to get our bodies in shape for the athletic event of childbirth. The more work we do now, hopefully the less labor you'll have later. So today, we're going to learn exercises that will tone your bodies and stretch your muscles. But before you do that, grab a pen or pencil, go to the back of your workbook and write down everything you ate yesterday."

The women in the group groaned.

"I know, I'm catching you off guard. And that's the point," Maddy told them. "We're going to get you on the right track with nutrition, too. But that's next week's class. Oh, and be honest, jot down everything you ate, even those chocolate brownies you had yesterday," she said. "I won't judge. I'm here to help."

The class, which was supposed to last an hour and a half, went quickly. Gracie was almost sorry it was over. She'd learned a lot, and actually felt a camaraderie with the others in the class.

"See you next week," one of the guys said to Sebastian. During the break, they'd bonded over football.

"Yeah, see ya."

Sebastian grabbed her yoga mat and took her hand. They walked over to the instructor. "Thank you," Gracie said. "It's a very informative class. I learned a lot."

"*We* learned a lot," Sebastian clarified.

The instructor shifted her gaze from her to Sebastian and smiled. "That's nice to hear. There's a lot to learn in a short time, and I'm afraid it can be overwhelming at times."

"Pregnancy is overwhelming. Period," Gracie admitted.

"You'll do fine. You have a good coach helping you. My number is in the workbook," Maddy said. "Call if you have any questions about the exercises or anything so far."

"Oh, we will," Sebastian assured her.

"Thanks again," Gracie said.

Once they were outside, Sebastian rubbed his stomach. "I think all these exercises made me hungry."

"Made *you* hungry?" She swatted his arm. "I did all the work!"

"Hey, it's not easy being the coach."

She chuckled, loving that she and Sebastian could finally have some light moments. "Are you complaining?"

"Never," he said, drawing her close. "Being by your side and helping you is my most important job."

Her head tilted to the side. "Really?"

"Yes, never doubt that."

As he leaned in, the deep green flecks in his eyes mesmerized her. And then his hands were cupping her face, his lips claiming hers. She fell into the kiss, right there in front of the birthing center, with cars driving by, for all the world to see.

Suddenly, she felt free, liberated from her doubts and fears.

Sebastian was her life, her future. She couldn't ask for more. And it dawned on her then how much she loved him, how much she needed him in her life.

She circled her arms around his neck. "How would you like to marry me?" Once the words were out, suddenly, she wanted nothing more.

"You want me to...to—"

She nodded. "Marry me."

Sebastian's eyes grew wide, and he backed away. She'd never seen that particular look on his face before, a mixture of disbelief and horror. As if this was the last thing on his mind, the last thing he wanted. And, oh, boy, she hadn't seen this coming. Not at all. Had she misread everything?

"Oh, God. I've shocked you."

"No, yes... I mean..."

Her eyes welled with tears. Sebastian didn't want her. He didn't love her. She'd misread all the signs.

Once again, she was that little girl on the outside, look-ing in. The woman who'd never quite be good enough for a Wingate, regardless of her big lottery win. She was only little Gracie Diaz, daughter of an immigrant ranch worker, someone not in his class, despite every-thing she'd accomplished in her life. All her innermost fears were coming true, slapping her in the face, break-ing her heart.

"Never mind," she said, turning and walking away.

"Gracie, wait."

"Sebastian, please stay where you are. Don't you dare follow me. I can and will take care of myself."

"You're mad and I'm sorry. I…uh…"

"I am not mad," she called over her shoulder, mak-ing a dash to her car. She was *humiliated*. How could she have been such a fool to think that Sebastian had fallen in love with her? He'd never said as much—he'd never actually confessed any true feelings for her at all. She'd only presumed. And what a faulty presumption that had been! All the while, he was only interested in the baby. He wanted to insure a place for himself in the baby's life, not hers. "Just leave me alone."

She picked up her pace, leaving him standing there, her dream man now her worst nightmare.

Gracie wiped at her teary eyes, unable to control her emotions tonight. She was confused and conflicted about what had happened earlier. Once she settled at her house, she made a cup of hot cocoa, got comfortable on the sofa and began to rethink things. It was remotely possible she'd overreacted with Sebastian today. He'd been calling and texting, but she wasn't ready to speak to him yet, and she figured, knowing him, that he just might show up on her doorstep tonight.

She didn't want that. It was the *last* thing she wanted. Not while she was so confused.

Maybe she'd sprung her proposal on him too soon. Just because she'd been sure of her feelings, it didn't mean that in that very moment, he was ready to make the same commitment. She'd been pushing him away almost all along, and then, suddenly, she'd done an about-face and decided she wanted to get married. She shook her head, trying to grasp the truth as the pain of his rejection gnawed away at her.

When the doorbell rang, she was both angry and hopeful. Maybe Sebastian had an explanation as to why he'd reacted that way and just maybe some of the blame could be from her highly emotional state. Had her hormones tripped to the moon and was she finally coming down to earth?

She wiped at her eyes again and went to the door.

And was taken totally by surprise, finding Lauren on her doorstep. "Lauren," she said, looking past her, seeing if anyone was with her. Her friend was alone and looking quite distraught.

"You've been crying," Lauren said. "I'm sorry. I ran over here as soon as I heard."

"You heard? Did Sebastian tell you what happened today?"

"Sebastian didn't say a word. I saw it on the news

tonight." Lauren wrapped her arms around her, hugging her tight. "I'm sorry. I'm sure there's a good explanation."

Gracie backed away. "You saw what on the news? I only just proposed to Sebastian this morning. How—"

"You *proposed*? That I didn't know. Oh, honey," she said, taking her hand. "Let's sit down."

Lauren tugged her over to the sofa in the living room and both took a seat.

"Are you going to tell me what you're talking about?"

"Maybe it's better if I showed you." Lauren took a tablet out of her purse and clicked a few times. "There's no easy way to explain this…so brace yourself."

Gracie trembled in anticipation. Lauren's expression alone was enough to make her shake with nerves. She bit her lip and gazed at the screen that loaded on the nightly news site. Under the entertainment and lifestyle section, there was Sebastian with his ex-girlfriend, supermodel Rhonda Pearson, in an embrace. The two looked very comfortable in each other's arms. And the next picture was of her and Sebastian, coming out of the birthing center, Sebastian holding her hand and her yoga mat. The headline read: "Wingate Love Triangle? Supermodel or Lottery Winner?"

Gracie's eyes traveled to the text below the photos and she whispered the words as she read them.

"With Wingate Enterprises still struggling, is Sebastian Wingate charming both mega wealthy women into investing in his company? Or is it true love? Which diva owns his heart? His ex-girlfriend, world-famous supermodel Rhonda Pearson, or his apparent baby mama, lottery winner and entrepreneur Gracie Diaz? Either way, Wingate is bound to come out a winner."

Gracie gasped as tears trickled down her face. She was numb, too stunned to feel anything at the moment. Her mind was spinning, and suddenly everything was beginning to make sense. Sebastian standing her up. Sebastian canceling dates at the last minute. Sebastian looking shocked when she proposed to him.

He wasn't at all the man she thought him to be. "I've been such a fool."

Lauren took her hand and squeezed. "It looks bad, Gracie. But I know Sebastian, and he's not capable of doing this to you."

"He's already done it, Lauren. Don't you see? He never wanted me. He wants his baby and his ex-girlfriend. He wants to have it all. And I can't figure out who's worse—him for betraying me and leading me on, or me, for believing I wasn't good enough for him. All my life I felt like I'd never fit into his world. My father worked for the family. He was loyal and dedicated, but he knew his place. I guess I didn't get that gene, because for just a while lately, I was beginning to believe that I was worthy of love, worthy of a Wingate. Now I see how wrong I've been. I'm not only worthy of Sebastian Wingate, I'm far better off without him."

Tears continued to stream down her face.

Lauren squeezed her hand tight. "Gracie, of course you're good enough for Sebastian. There was never any doubt, but I hate that you're writing him off without getting an explanation from him."

"How do you explain the photo, then? Look at them together. He doesn't look like a man who's ready to commit to another woman."

"Gracie, I'm so sorry this happened."

"S-so…am…I." She put her hand over her tummy and thought of the baby she was to have. Sebastian's child. Her heart shattered at the realization that this child wouldn't have the comfort and security of a real family unit. Originally, she'd wanted to have the baby alone, to raise her child as she saw fit. But when Sebastian entered into the picture, she'd started to believe they could become a true family. That dream was way out of her reach now.

She sighed deeply, trying to hold tight to her emotions, but her tears flowed freely and she couldn't stop them. The ache inside was greater than anything she'd experienced before.

"The a-article s-says that Wingate Enterprises is still h-having money troubles. You and I have talked about this, but I thought maybe things had gotten better… since, since Sebastian never once mentioned it to me."

Lauren shook her head. "Don't think it, Gracie. Sebastian wouldn't use you that way."

Her heart broken, Gracie didn't agree. "Apparently, the news report says differently."

A pounding at her door startled them both. Lauren rose to peer out the window. "It's him," she said. "Sebastian is here."

"I don't want to talk to him."

"Are you sure, honey?"

"I'm sure. I can't, not tonight." Maybe never. "I'm too upset."

"He's a hard one to say no to, but I'll try."

"I don't want to see him or hear his voice now. I'll be in the kitchen."

"Okay, I'll deal with him."

Gracie rose up on wobbly legs and went into the kitchen. She slumped in the chair and waited. A few moments later, she heard muffled sounds from the front door, but thankfully she couldn't make out what they were saying. A long time passed and finally Lauren entered the kitchen. "He's gone. It took some doing. I finally used the baby card, telling him your stomach is already upset and seeing you might jeopardize the baby's health. That got him to leave."

"Good. Thank you."

"He's really hurting, too, Gracie. He says none of it's true."

"What else could he say?"

"He asked me to make sure you're all right. He's genuinely concerned."

For the baby. Not her. The fact remained that he seemed totally horrified when she'd asked him to marry her. That pain just added to the humiliation of seeing him with his ex, of the entire county seeing her in that light. Of basically announcing to the world that Sebastian was the true father of her baby.

How could she forgive any of that?

Lauren began opening cupboards, looking for things. "What are you doing?"

"I'm going to make you some herbal tea. And you need to eat something. I bet you haven't put anything in your stomach for most of the day."

"You'd be right. But I don't think I can eat a morsel right now."

"Tea, then. And I'll make you some soup. If you're hungry later, it'll be waiting for you."

"Thanks, tea sounds good."

Lauren made herself comfortable in the kitchen. It came second nature with her, and there was no doubt whatever she made would turn out delicious. "Thanks for staying with me. I really appreciate it."

"Of course. I'm not leaving until you feel better."

"Oh, then you'll be taking up permanent residency?"

Lauren's shoulders slumped and sympathy filled her eyes.

"I'm sorry. Bad joke. I'll be okay. I just have to…to… I don't know." She sighed. After being with Sebastian these last few weeks, she'd grown so much closer to him. They'd gone beyond the physical. Great sex was one thing, but she thought they'd really made a connection in other ways. They'd had fun together and had a possible future to look forward to. And she'd finally allowed herself the freedom to fall in love with him. That was what hurt the most, the betrayal of her trust. When it had been the hardest thing for her to give.

When the tea was ready and a delicious-smelling vegetable soup was simmering on the stovetop, Lauren took a seat at the table, handing her a teacup. It was a cinnamon-spicy blend perfect for winter and warmed her throat going down. "This is good."

"Hmm. It is."

"Lauren?"

"Yeah?"

Gracie steadied her breathing, trying to calm herself down. "What can you tell me about Sebastian's relationship with Rhonda?"

"Well, I don't know much really. Sutton said that it wasn't what it seemed. But Sebastian's pretty closed-mouth about his relationships."

"Do you think Rhonda broke his heart?"

"That, I honestly don't know," Lauren admitted. "It's something you could find out, when you're ready to speak to Sebastian again."

A lump rose to Gracie's throat. "Will I ever be ready?"

"Well, you're having his child, so I would think at some point you're going to have to be, but you don't have to think about that now. Just sip your tea and try to relax."

"I'll try."

But Gracie knew sleep would be a long time coming tonight. Her heart ached and she didn't figure that was going to get better anytime soon.

Sebastian was up half the night, pacing the floor, wearing out the rug, as his mother would say. He sipped bourbon straight up, too anxious to sleep, too keyed up to think about anything but Gracie and how she was feeling.

Tonight, when he'd gone to Gracie's house, Lauren had laid down the law. Gracie didn't want to hear from him; she didn't want to see him. And how could he blame her? He'd lied to her, omitted the truth and subsequently destroyed the relationship they'd been building. She'd actually proposed to him, and it had taken him by total surprise. He'd reacted badly, and he didn't think he'd ever get the hurt look on Gracie's face out of his head.

But he hadn't hurt her on purpose, damn it, and he was innocent of the claims the news reports had made. There was no love triangle. He *loved* Gracie. And it'd taken him losing her to figure out just how much she meant to him. Suddenly it was all clear, but she wouldn't believe him now if he declared his love.

Rhonda wasn't back in his life, and the innuendo that he was using either woman to bankroll his business had struck him right between the eyes. Nothing was further from the truth. But how could he ever convince Gracie of that?

When his cell phone rang at midnight, he had an iota of hope it was Gracie. But his hope was stifled the second Rhonda's image appeared on his screen. He let it ring a few times, and then finally picked up.

"I'm so sorry," she said immediately.

This wasn't her fault. Other than the fact that she was world-famous and always had some sort of paparazzi following her if they sniffed out a story. But he should've realized that. He should've known that would be the case. Even in Royal. "I had no idea I was being followed. I only wanted to help Lonny, Sebastian. I never meant to hurt you."

"I know that, Rhonda. And I wanted to help him, too. My mistake is that I wasn't honest with Gracie."

"You really care about her, don't you?" she asked softly.

"Yeah, and she's not talking to me right now."

"She's having your baby. I guess I should say congratulations. There's no doubt you'll make a great father, Sebastian."

"Thanks," he said. "But right now I have to figure out a way to gain Gracie's trust."

"Let me know if I can help in any way."

He didn't think bringing Rhonda into this would help. It could possibly make things worse. No, he had to do this on his own. But first he had to get Gracie to talk to him.

# Nine

Gracie lay low for the next few days. She didn't want to see anyone, and she certainly didn't want to do an interview. News vans had parked outside her house for two days, but by the third day, they'd found the next new big scandal and left. Thanks to Sebastian and his lies, she'd been like a prisoner in her own home. The flowers he sent every day had been returned, the notes went unopened. Sebastian continued to text her, continued to clog up her voice mail with messages, until finally, because he'd given her no choice, she decided to confront him.

On Friday morning, she put her long dark hair up in a ponytail, and tossed on a ball cap and sunglasses. Wearing jeans and a big bulky sweater and no makeup, she got into her car, making sure no one was following her, and drove to Sebastian's office on the outskirts of town.

She parked in the large parking lot and sat there, determined to set him straight, make her point and get away from him as quickly as possible. But her heart still ached, and it was difficult to make the move, difficult to get out of the car.

"You're doing the right thing, Gracie," she whispered to herself. She had to put the future she'd always dreamed about out of her mind. Had to make a clean break. Sebastian would be free to date anyone he wanted. She'd make that clear, too. Just thinking of the humiliating photos and articles written about her gave her the incentive she needed to get out of the car and march toward Sebastian's office. As luck or fate would have it, she was nearing the building when she heard her name called from behind.

"Gracie? Is that you?"

She turned to find a blonde-haired, green-eyed Wingate approaching. For a second, she thought it was Sutton, but as he strode closer, she knew it was definitely not him. She'd learned the tiny nuances that other people usually didn't notice to determine it was Sebastian.

He seemed glad to see her, his eyes so very green at the moment, his handsome face filled with hope. A less determined woman might just melt on the spot, but she wouldn't allow that to happen. If she had to confront Sebastian in the parking lot, so be it.

She acknowledged him with a nod.

"Gracie, I've been trying to reach you for days."

"I guess I didn't want to be reached, Sebastian."

"I'm sorry about this whole mess. If you'll let me explain, I'll—"

"I don't want to hear your explanations, Sebastian. I doubt I'd believe them. I only came here to tell you we're through. You can stop sending flowers and notes. They don't mean anything to me." She took a breath, watching the light dim in his eyes, watching his demeanor change instantly.

"You're not even going to hear me out?" he rasped.

"Are you saying you didn't lie to me countless times?"

"I—I… Okay I did, but for a good reason."

"There's no reason that's good enough for me," Gracie said adamantly. "I'm sorry. I don't want to see you anymore. I think it's best this way."

"It's *not* best. You can't break up with me like this. You have to be reasonable and allow me to explain."

His voice held an edge, as if he was barely holding on to his anger. She knew why he was so upset, aside from being caught in the act. It was because of the baby. He wanted an heir, his own flesh and blood, but he didn't want her. Sebastian had never claimed to love her. He'd rebuffed her marriage proposal almost instantly, making her feel unworthy yet again. And worst of all, he may have pursued her solely for her money.

She lifted her chin, more determined now to make things clear. "I won't get in the way of you seeing the baby, Sebastian. I'm not that cruel. You'll have generous visitation rights. The child should know its father.

We'll work something out between our attorneys when the time comes."

"We'll work something out between our attorneys," he repeated, his voice a low growl. "That's not the way we should approach this, and you know it, Gracie."

"I know of no other way."

A muscle ticked in his jaw. "I can think of a dozen different ways, and they all start with you letting me explain."

"Ever since we've met, I've listened to your explanations, Sebastian. I've heard about enough this time." She released a quavering breath. "I'm humiliated and hurt and angry enough to cut you completely out of my life. Am I sorry about this? Yes, but it's not my doing. It's yours."

Sebastian closed his eyes briefly. "We can't be through."

His plea broke her heart all over again. "You're free to see anyone you want. You can go about your business and—"

"I don't want to see anyone else! Damn it, Gracie, listen to me. I have no feelings for Rhonda—"

"Stop. Just stop, Sebastian. No more. I have to think about the baby and how this turmoil is affecting my pregnancy. If I do know one thing, it's that you care about this child. At least, I think so."

"Of course I do," he said firmly.

"F-fine, then. If you care about the health of this baby, let me walk away. I need you to. This is hard for me, Sebastian. Maybe you don't realize how much, but

I've let you hurt me enough. I can't do it any longer. I don't have the strength."

Sebastian stared at her, his gaze penetrating, and she recognized the exact moment he relented. His face fell, his shoulders slumped and he shifted his stance ever so slightly to let her pass.

She stepped away from him and squeezed her eyes closed, saying a silent goodbye to her dream. Her heart hurt now, more than it ever had. Putting one foot in front of the other, she moved through the parking lot, got into her car, took one last look at Sebastian and then drove off. She was doing what she had to do to protect herself and the baby, yet the pain was almost unbearable.

It was hard to believe that just a week ago, Gracie had proposed marriage to him and he, like a fool, had reacted badly. It wasn't that he didn't love her, he did. He was just coming to the realization that Gracie was his whole world, when she'd proposed and caught him off guard. Now that she'd cut him out of her life, it was a vital wound to his heart, a stabbing pain that ached with every breath he took.

But he loved her beyond belief and he wasn't about to let her go so easily. He'd just have to show her she couldn't get rid of him so fast. That he was in it for the long haul. So he mustered his bravado and entered the birthing center, enduring the stares of the couples who now knew more about him than he'd like. But he was here for Gracie and their baby.

He waited around for Gracie, hoping to prove to her

he wasn't going to abandon her, but after a few minutes, the instructor, Maddy, approached him. "Hello again."

"Hi."

"I, um, thought I'd mention," she said quietly, just for his ears, "your partner, Ms. Diaz, dropped out of class."

"She did?"

"Yes, she's going to be taking private classes from now on. I'm sorry."

"No, no. I should've figured. I'm sorry for bringing your place into the public eye like that. It was all one big misunderstanding."

She nodded. "It's okay. Good luck with the baby," she said.

"Thank you."

Sebastian walked out of the place feeling like he'd been sucker punched in the gut. He was angry with Gracie for cutting him out of her life like that, but he was angrier with himself for all the bumbling mistakes he'd made with her. Of course she wouldn't want to show her face in the early bird class, not after all the things that had been printed about her.

She been humiliated, and it had been his fault.

He'd never really given her a reason to trust him. He'd gone about this courtship all wrong, and wow, now he was paying the price.

By six o'clock he was dressed in jeans and a button-down shirt and knocking on his mother's door. It was family dinner time, his mother calling the shots, wanting everyone in the family to sit down with her. She didn't do this often, but when she did, you didn't dare refuse. He was in no mood tonight for a get-together, but his family's name, once again, had been dragged through the mud because of some overambitious news reports that got it all wrong. He owed his family an explanation, for many things.

Ava greeted him at the door with a big hug, and the look in her eyes wasn't what he'd expected. She'd always been a stickler for transparency and expected to be clued in on everything that went on with the family. It surprised him that she wasn't showing her disapproval. She wasn't judging him, but instead was providing unconditional love. "Hello, dear."

"Mom."

"How are you doing tonight? You had a rough week."

"I did, but I'm doing okay."

"Just okay?" Ava asked.

"I may have lost something, *someone*, who I really care about. Mom."

"That's not the man I raised, Sebastian. You're one to never give up, and it's a trait I admire about you. Don't throw in the towel just yet. Gracie will come around."

He doubted that, but his mother's encouragement meant a great deal to him.

"Come, your brothers and sisters are all here."

She led him into the dining room, where the others were already seated, noisily chattering while drinking wine and munching on appetizers. "Hey," he said to everyone, slapping his brothers' backs and kissing the women on the cheek.

Sutton and Lauren were here along with Beth and

Cam, who were back from their honeymoon. Miles and Chloe were in town, as was Aunt Piper, who was sitting beside Brian. Beside them sat their cousins and the women in their lives, Luke and Kelly and Zeke and Reagan. Then, turning toward his baby sister, Sebastian marveled at what an adorable threesome Harley and Grant and little Daniel made. Soon, Daniel would have a cousin, which was a good thing, but would they be close? Would they even get a chance to know each other?

He pulled out a chair and sat down. This dining room in his mother's rental apartment was a far cry from the beautifully decorated oversize one in the mansion they were used to, but it didn't matter. The family was here, and everyone was in good spirits.

After downing a glass of wine, he asked for everyone's attention and apologized to his family. "I'm sorry for bringing our name down again. We've worked so hard to improve our image, but I have to say the news reports and tabloids got it mostly wrong."

"They usually do," Miles said, and others in the room nodded. Being wealthy and famous meant there was a target on your back, and he'd never felt it more than this past year.

"The truth is, Gracie and I *are* going to have a baby. That part was factual. But I only just found out the baby was mine. I guess everyone assumed she'd gotten pregnant through an in vitro procedure, but as Grant knows, the treatments never got that far."

Grant smiled. "My lips are sealed."

As any good doctor would say.

"I'm sorry that you all had to find that out on the news. I wanted to shout it out to the world, but Gracie wanted to wait."

He was met with a round of congratulations and smiles, which bolstered his sagging heart.

His family really had his back, and he needed that right now.

"*The Gossiper* wasn't too kind, either." Sutton had been furious about what that sleazy tabloid had written. "They can all go to—" He stopped himself, realizing Daniel was in the room.

"Thanks, bro. But just so you know, I wasn't going behind Gracie's back with Rhonda. I was trying to help her with her brother, Lonny. My mistake was in not telling Gracie about it."

"Why didn't you?" Lauren asked.

He turned to her. "Lonny was heading down a bad path. He'd gotten in trouble at school and was acting out. And since I'd always bonded with the boy, Rhonda simply asked me to talk to Lonny. He valued my friendship and needed some guidance, and Rhonda asked me to keep this private. If news got out, she feared it would set back any progress I made with the boy.

"Now I might've blown it for good with Gracie. It's killing me that she won't talk to me. I should've been up front with her. I should've trusted her with what I was doing, and now *she* doesn't trust me." Regret tightened the corners of his mouth. "And the worst part? I honestly don't know if there's anything I can do at this point to change her mind. Anyway, this isn't a Sebastian pity party. I just wanted my family to finally know the truth."

They nodded and gave words of encouragement, which meant a lot to him.

And after another round of drinks, Miles spoke up. "Well, I have good news to report, and I'm glad we're all together today to hear it. Thanks to Chloe's heads-up, I finally have proof that dear 'Uncle' Keith did more embezzling than we originally thought. Turns out that while Dad was recovering from his stroke, Keith took advantage of the crisis to siphon off huge chunks of money without us realizing it. And the best news is, the money is all accounted for and we'll have it back in our hands soon. It's enough to keep our other holdings afloat and enough to put the family back on track financially."

"That's wonderful news," Ava said. "I still can't believe I let that crook dupe me for so long. Brian, I'm sorry to say that in front of you, but we all know you're not like your uncle Keith."

"He certainly is not," Aunt Piper said in defense of her much younger boyfriend. Brian might be a Cooper but it was in name only. He'd proven his loyalty to the family by helping to expose his traitorous uncle.

"Miles, you've really saved our family," Ava said, with pride in her eyes. Miles had once been the black sheep of the family, but he'd come around, and his firm, Steel Security, was a top-notch investigative company.

"Thanks, Mother. But it was all of us. We're all in

this together, the good, the bad, the ugly. And it's been ugly, but all that's behind us now."

"Yes," Ava said. "We've proven time and again that we're a family that sticks together."

"It's really great news because," Luke said, taking his fiancée Kelly's hand, "now Kelly and I can go to Oahu and get the hotel ready for the big launch without worrying about the family. We plan to spend an entire month there, and having this peace of mind will help take some of the pressure off."

"Pressure in paradise?" Harley asked. She and Grant were leaving in just a matter of days themselves, and so this family dinner was also a good way to send them off.

"I know, it's tough work, but somebody's got to do it," Kelly teased. The family's mood was definitely lightening up. It was good to see.

"Well, since this is a day for announcements, Reagan and I have some good news, too. Seems Sebastian isn't the only one bringing a new little one into the world."

All eyes turned to Luke's brother, Zeke, and Reagan. "While we're in San Diego setting up the new family-oriented resort there, we'll be also using the facilities for our own little ready-made family." He looked to Reagan. "Tell them, honey."

Reagan didn't hesitate. "We're having twins!"

Gasps of joy filled the room. Everyone rose to congratulate Zeke and Reagan, and Sebastian was incredibly happy for them. Seems his family was finally blessed with good news. It only made him wish for a second chance with Gracie. Or was that a third or fourth? He'd certainly messed up his chances.

And after everyone was settled back in their seats, Brian stood up with glass in hand. "I'd like to propose a toast."

The room quieted and all eyes were on Brian Cooper at the opposite end of the table. "But first I have something to say. I can't tell you how sorry I am about what my uncle did to Wingate Enterprises. It was unforgivable and I'm truly glad he's out of all our lives now. But I'm also grateful that despite everything, all of you have welcomed me into your homes and family." He cleared his throat. "And since this is a day for announcements, I'd like to add to the happiness. Ava," he said, garnering her full attention, "you're going to be an aunt again."

His mother's mouth just about dropped to the floor. Her eyes riveted to her sister, Piper.

And Piper acknowledged her with an excited nod of the head.

"Yes, it's true." Piper took Brian's hand and rose, moving to stand beside him. "We didn't want to steal anyone's thunder today. But yes, Brian and I are having a baby. We'll think about a wedding some time down the line, but right now we're excited for this child."

His mother walked over to Aunt Piper. "You robbed the cradle," she said. The entire family watched on with trepidation. Ava and Piper hadn't always been close, so everyone's eyes were on his mother. "Lucky you," she declared finally, wrapping her arms around her sister and hugging her to her chest. "Congratulations," she murmured, turning to kiss Brian's cheek. "May I finish the toast?" she asked him.

He handed her the glass and took a step back. Ava began, "This family...well, we've been through a lot, and I can't say it's always been pleasant. But we survived and are stronger for it. So this toast is for each and every one of you and the new little ones to arrive soon. May we always be close, be loyal, be true. May this family not only survive, but *thrive*. Here's to our family," Ava said, her eyes misting up as she raised her glass.

Glasses clinked, and there were heartwarming smiles all around.

Now, if only Gracie were here by his side, all would be perfect.

# Ten

Keeping busy was the only thing keeping Gracie sane at the moment. She'd never felt lonelier in her life. She moved around her house as if in slow motion, thinking back on her time with Sebastian. They'd had something pretty wonderful together that only lasted mere days, but it had been gut-wrenchingly powerful, and now it was gone. He'd stopped calling and texting as she'd asked. It only made her feel hollow inside and so incredibly sad.

Had Sebastian moved on already?

Had he given up on her?

It wasn't that she wanted to speak to him, but if she was being totally honest, a part of her wanted to know he was suffering as much as she was. She wanted to know that he felt the same emptiness. Was that self-ish of her?

Why couldn't things just go back to the way they were before?

When her doorbell rang, she quickly opened the door to Beth. "Hi, I'm a little early."

"That's no problem. I'm happy to see you."

"Same here."

They hugged a little longer than usual, Gracie needing the support. She'd called Beth this morning and they'd spoken about her honeymoon with Cam, which had been fabulous. Gracie wanted to explain to Beth about the baby and why she hadn't told her that Sebastian was the father. It was a misstep on her part and she apologized. Luckily, Beth hadn't taken offense. Then they'd lamented about how much they missed seeing each other, and Gracie had invited her over. "Come in. I made lunch for us."

"Something wildly Mexican and tasty?"

"Your favorite. Enchiladas. Come into the kitchen."

It was great having her friend here now, filling the empty void in her heart for a little while. She led Beth into her modest kitchen. "Tea, lemonade, wine? What can I get you to drink?"

"I'd love some tea, Gracie, and if you don't mind me saying so, you look…"

"Terrible, I know."

"No, you could never look terrible. But you're stressed, aren't you?"

She gave her a half smile. "A bit."

"I thought so."

Beth took her hand. "I'm worried about you."

"Don't be, Beth. You know I'll bounce back. I always do."

Beth gave her a skeptical look. "Nice try, Gracie, but this is me and I know you better than that. You're hurting."

She shrugged and offered her friend a seat. "I'll be fine...eventually." She didn't really think so, not with the way she'd been feeling lately, but it sounded good.

Gracie warmed a pot of tea on the stove and then picked up a pair of pot holders and took the dish of enchiladas out of the oven.

"Oh, those smell delish. Can I help with anything?"

"No, thanks. I'm good." She poured two cups of tea and then placed a salad on the table.

"You're a busy bee to keep your mind off...things. I recognize the traits, Gracie. I'm a lot like that, too."

"Guilty as charged." She dished up the enchiladas, steam rising up off the cheesy topping, and set the plates down on the table. "Here we go."

"Those look wonderful. My mouth is watering."

"Let's dig in. Baby is hungry, too."

Beth's eyes softened immediately as she gazed down at Gracie's belly. "Did you know that you're in good company? We had a family dinner the other night and found out that Aunt Piper is pregnant, too. And so are Zeke and Reagan—those two are having twins, for heaven's sakes. I can't keep up with my family."

Gracie smiled. "I know. That's very good news.

Babies bring so much joy. Your family is expanding, isn't it?"

"Yeah, it sure is. Only thing is, Sebastian looks about as frazzled as you do. He's hurting, too, Gracie. He told the family about what happened and apologized for bringing the family's image down again, but none of it is true. He has a good explanation for all of it."

Gracie picked up her fork, and wished Beth would do the same. She was sorry Beth had to find out about the baby through some sleazy tabloid article; she'd wanted to tell her friend herself. But as far as Sebastian was concerned, she didn't want to hear it. She'd never forget the way he'd reacted to her marriage proposal, and if that wasn't her first clue, then him seeing his ex-girlfriend behind her back certainly was. Add in that his company needed cash to completely get out of the red, and she had a rock-solid case of no-can-do.

"I really don't want to talk about Sebastian, if you don't mind."

"I, uh, sure. All I'm going to say is to please think about giving the guy a chance to explain. And now," she said, making a zipping gesture over her mouth, "I promise, no more talk about my brother."

"Thank you," Gracie said. "I'm not a horrible person, you know, but I've been hurt and…"

Beth took her hand. "I get it. We won't talk about it. I'm not judging you. And I'm here if you need me."

"I know you are."

Beth finally dug into her food. She made a satisfied face and sighed quietly as she chewed. "This is heaven."

"I'm glad you like it. It's a foolproof recipe, handed down from my grandmother."

"I love that you're keeping your family traditions alive like that. It's special."

"I do try whenever I can," Gracie said.

"You should be a chef specializing in Mexican cuisine."

"No, I think I'll leave that to Lauren, thank you very much. Actually, I wanted to pick your brain about something else. If you're up to it."

"Sure. What's up?" Beth asked.

"Well, I'm still hoping to become an event planner and open up my own business. I've been looking for a space to lease or buy. But since you're an expert at it, would you mind giving me pointers and tips on getting started? I think I have pregnancy brain."

"That *is* a thing."

"Oh, how well I know it!" she said. "So maybe you can clear up some questions I have and we can go from there."

"Okay, sure. And, Gracie, just for the record, I think it's admirable that you want to pursue your dream. I know you'll be a success and a great mommy, too."

"That's my goal."

"Okay, so ask away."

It was almost three o'clock before they finished their talk and Beth left. Gracie felt inspired after getting her questions answered. Beth had a wealth of knowledge in the event-planning department. She'd planned so many Wingate parties and charity events in her life, and was generous in sharing the business side of it, as well. With her mind spinning in several directions, Gracie got lost in thought. And so when the doorbell rang again, it took her a few seconds to realize someone was at her door.

"Just a minute," she said. Gracie had given her house-keeper the day off, which had worked out perfectly since she needed to keep busy, and cooking and cleaning had done the trick.

She opened the door and stared into the striking blue-green eyes of supermodel Rhonda Pearson. Her first inclination was to slam the door in her face. But she wouldn't do that.

"I know, I'm probably the last person on earth you wanted to see."

They'd never met before, yet the woman assumed she knew who she was. Well, yes, she *was* that famous.

"I'm Rhonda." She put out her hand.

Gracie shook it once—she hated her manners at times. "Gracie."

"May I come in?"

She really wasn't up to this. "It depends."

"Before you think otherwise, Sebastian has no idea I'm here. I guess you could say I'm here at my own risk. He'd actually murder me in my sleep if he found out I came to speak with you."

Gracie had had a fleeting notion to do the same to the two of them when she'd seen them in that cozy scene on the news. It had knocked her for a loop. "And why is that?"

"Can I please come in? I'd love to explain everything."

Gracie sighed. So many people had encouraged her to hear Sebastian out, but maybe this was the next best thing. "Yes, please. Come inside."

She showed Rhonda to her living room and offered her a seat.

"Thank you," the other woman said.

Gracie nodded, took a seat, too, and continued to stare at the gorgeous supermodel. Rhonda's features were picture-perfect, with big turquoise eyes, long, luscious blond hair and a figure that wouldn't ever know a bad fit.

Rhonda seemed confident in her own skin and didn't seem to mind Gracie's staring. It was as if she expected it, which wasn't so much conceited as it was honest. She banked her life on her good looks, flawless skin and body. "So tell me exactly why you are here."

"That's easy to answer. I'm here for Sebastian. One good turn deserves another. Even though he would hate that I came here."

"Yes, you've said that already."

"You see, I'm raising my younger brother, Lonny. And when Sebastian and I were together, Lonny became attached to him. They really got along great. Sebastian was such a good role model to Lonny, and my brother was at his best around Sebastian. Only, when my relationship with Sebastian ended, I thought a clean break would be best for Lonny. But that apparently was totally wrong. Sebastian lost touch with Lonny, mostly because of me. And because his company started having trouble. I didn't realize how much Sebastian meant to Lonny until he started acting out."

Rhonda sighed. "Let's face it, it's not easy having your big sister modeling bathing suits all over magazine covers and being under the scrutiny of the paparazzi. Lonny is at a sensitive age. I mean, do you remember when you were fifteen? It's tough. And there's tons of peer pressure. Anyway, when I came back to town recently to give Lonny a good home life, his rebellion didn't end. It got worse. So I called Sebastian and asked for his help. I knew he could get through to him."

"You're saying Sebastian was meeting you secretly for Lonny's sake?"

"Yes, and it's all my fault he didn't confide in you. I made him promise not to tell a soul, in order to protect my brother. If news got out about him getting into trouble, the paparazzi would've damaged him, permanently, I'm afraid."

"Sebastian lied to me about where he was."

"If he did, I'm sorry. But you see, he bailed Lonny out of a jam. My brother got in with the wrong crowd, and the boys vandalized a building. He could've gone to jail if Sebastian didn't convince him to own up to what he did. Lonny confessed and Sebastian pulled some strings to get a judge to give Lonny a second chance."

"He did?" It was too complicated a scenario to not be true. Gracie could actually see Sebastian helping a young boy out that way. But if she was to believe that, she wished he would've trusted her with the truth.

Rhonda nodded. "Yes, and I'm very grateful to him, but we're only friends now, Gracie. I swear it."

"You broke his heart. I think he'd care more for you than just as a friend."

Sebastian's ex shook her head. "I didn't break his heart. I never wanted out of our relationship. *He* broke up with me, and he let me save face with the public by claiming I broke up with him. It was silly of me to do that, but Sebastian went along with it for my sake. You see, he's a really good guy."

Gracie pulled air into her lungs. "It's a lot to take in."

"I know, but whatever the press wanted you to believe about me and Sebastian isn't true. And if you'll allow me, let me show you something."

"What?"

Rhonda pulled out her cell phone and scrolled until she found what she'd been looking for. "Here we go. Just hit the arrow for the video." She handed Gracie the phone and she turned the video on. She seemed to be watching a track-and-field event.

"That's Lonny. He's on the track team now in high school. He's always been fast and he loves to run. A short time ago, he might've landed in juvenile detention, but look at him now. He won the race and the coach is very impressed with him. With Sebastian's guidance and a little encouragement from his big sister, Lonny is the happiest I've seen him."

The impact of this wasn't lost on Gracie. She'd known boys who hadn't been that lucky and had gotten into major trouble, only to drop out of school. She had a brother, too, and only wanted the best for Enrico. Just like Rhonda wanted for her younger brother. "This is wonderful to see."

"It is. The only drawback is that you and Sebastian aren't together anymore. And I feel responsible for that."

"It's not your fault. Sebastian is the one who made the mistakes."

"Everyone is worthy of a second chance. Lonny got one, and hopefully Sebastian will, too. Please think about it. Oh, and congratulations on the baby. I know you both will make wonderful parents."

Hope jetted through Gracie's heart. She'd refused Sebastian's explanations because she'd been extremely hurt. She'd lumped all of his mistakes and her misgivings into one tidy package and labeled it "Unforgivable," and she hadn't thought anything he said would be enough to change her mind.

And now, thanks to a supermodel and a fifteen-year-old kid, she had a better understanding of why Sebastian had done what he'd done. "Th-thank you. And you don't have to worry. Sebastian won't know a thing about this."

"So you'll give him a second chance?"

"I'll think about it."

"Good." Rhonda smiled and glanced at her watch. "I'd better go. I promised Lonny we'd go out for ice cream after his practice today, but he wanted a protein shake instead. I'm so proud of him."

The winsome look on her face filled Gracie's heart. It was as if both of them were getting a fresh start. "You don't want to be late. And thank you, Rhonda. I do appreciate your honesty."

Gracie walked her out and watched her drive off in a sporty silver car, her heavy heart easing a bit learning of Sebastian's motives.

In just two hours, Gracie had a private early bird childbirth class. She closed her eyes and concentrated on that, instead of the eye-opening conversation she'd just had with Sebastian's ex-girlfriend. Gracie sighed, afraid to hope, but even more afraid, not to hope.

The next day, Gracie dressed in a black wool blazer and slacks, with a cozy blue cashmere sweater underneath to keep her warm. The weather had turned nasty, the clouds overhead gloomy. It would've been a good day to stay in, but she'd done enough of that lately. She wasn't about to mope all day. She'd had a very informative childbirth class at her home last night, when the instructor, Maddy, had let it slip that Sebastian had also hired her for a private class. Maddy had kind eyes, and there was a soothing softness in her voice as she spoke. Perhaps she was a bit of a matchmaker. So Gracie didn't call her out on the possible intentional slip but instead questioned Maddy on why she supposed he'd done that. And the woman had simply replied, "He wants to support you when the baby comes."

Every time Gracie thought about that, the frost in her heart thawed a bit. Heck, who was she kidding? She was melting inside, and all signs pointed to Sebastian being a good guy. Still, she couldn't fathom why he'd rejected her marriage proposal.

She headed to The Eatery, opting to do some work this morning. A frigid wind swept her inside and she took off her blazer and weaved her fingers through her tangled hair. She glanced inside the work area, and found Lauren and Sutton, apparently in a private moment.

Quietly, she moved into the back room, giving them privacy.

"Is that you, Gracie?" Lauren called out.

"Don't mind me," she called back. "Go back to what you two were doing."

Lauren walked into the back room and they came face-to-face. "We weren't doing anything other than talking. How are you, Gracie? What are you doing here so early?"

It *was* early for her. She usually didn't start working on the books until nine, and it was only seven thirty. "I, uh, just had to get out of my house. I couldn't sleep, and well, I guess I needed a friend."

Lauren put out her arms, and she walked straight into them. "You've got a friend right here."

"Thank you." Tears came to her eyes. Lauren's friendship meant so much to her.

"Is it about Sebastian?"

She nodded. "I love him, Lauren. And I think I've made a terrible mistake. I'm not sure about anything anymore."

"It's a confusing time."

"It is," Gracie said hoarsely.

"But if you know you love him, why not hear him out?"

"I know, I should." She pulled back to search Lauren's eyes. "Right? Everyone's been telling me to give him another chance…"

"I think you should."

"So do I." The deep voice came from behind and she turned to find Sebastian there. Immediately her heart started pumping hard. "Sorry, I overheard." Then he smiled.

"What on earth?" Gracie looked at Lauren.

She shrugged. "I guess you thought I was with Sutton."

"You know I did!"

"Sebastian came by to talk, the same way you did just now. It seems like kismet that you were on the same page, and we all know this mistaken-identity thing can get really baffling." Lauren gave her an innocent look. "So I guess I'll leave you two alone now."

Dumbfounded, she stared after Lauren, watching her leave the room, and feeling Sebastian's overwhelming presence in the room.

And when she finally turned to meet his eyes, he wouldn't stop smiling.

Her lips curled up, as well. She was glad to see him, too. Even if the twin-switch mistake had happened to her once again. Couldn't one of them style their hair differently or something? They looked identical, and she wasn't really thinking that Sebastian would come to talk to Lauren so early in the morning. So when she'd first walked in, she'd assumed it was Sutton.

"I've missed you, Gracie."

She nodded, unable to speak at the moment. He'd heard everything. And she wasn't angry or embarrassed about it. She was glad. Yes, *glad* that her feelings for him were finally out in the open. She'd been sheltering her emotions for too long. It wasn't healthy, and now she felt liberated. "I've missed you, too."

"There's a lot I want to say to you, but not here. Will you have dinner with me tonight? I want to take you someplace special."

She smiled. "Yes."

Sebastian took a big gulp of air and sighed in relief. The look on his face was filled with gratitude and promise. "I'll pick you up at six."

"I'll be ready."

He grinned. "Until tonight, then."

And he leaned over to kiss her cheek, leaving her to wonder just what he had in store for her tonight.

Gracie could hardly concentrate on what she was doing. Sitting in the back room at the computer, she opened and closed the inventory app for The Eatery half a dozen times, her hands shaking. Excitement and curiosity crowded her mind to the point that there was literally no room inside her head for anything else.

"Why don't you quit for the day," Lauren said, coming to stand beside her at the desk. "You're not going to be able to get anything accomplished today."

Gracie ran her hands down her face. "I think you're right. My heart's not in it right now."

"That's because your heart is where it should be. With Sebastian."

Gracie tilted her head toward Lauren. "Thanks to you."

"Sure, I'll take credit if you want to give it to me. But you have to know that I had no idea Sebastian was coming over to speak to me until early this morning, when he texted me. I think Sutton put him up to it. He said his brother was pretty desperate and needed to talk it out with someone close to Gracie. Me."

"Really?"

"Yes, really. The guy's nuts about you. And when you opened up to me this morning, I couldn't know that he'd overheard. But I'm glad he did. You two have been dancing around each other for weeks now."

"True story." She was ready now to hear Sebastian out. After her conversation with Rhonda, she was ready to give him the benefit of the doubt and try to move forward. Finally admitting that she was in love with him, saying it aloud to Lauren, made it all seem real and attainable. At least, she was willing to give it a try.

"So go home, gussy up and have a good night with Sebastian."

"That sounds like a plan," Gracie said. "Are you sure you don't need me?"

"I'm covered here, and the inventory can wait. Just go." Lauren was already handing Gracie her blazer. "Keep warm, it's cold out there."

"The baby's keeping me warm." Which was true. Being pregnant had some advantages, like she was never too cold. The added weight and her hormones kept her from turning into a popsicle during the winter season. "You should try it sometime."

"The Eatery's my baby right now. But someday in the future, our children will be playing with each other. I'm sure of it."

"That's a beautiful thought. Thanks again." She hugged Lauren. Their friendship was rock-solid. Lauren and Beth had given Gracie nothing but support lately. She was lucky to have both women in her life right now.

One hour later, Gracie was home, soaking in a nice hot bath. Her nerves were so rattled she'd lit candles and put on her favorite soft country rock music before stepping into the tub. The only thing missing in the bubbles was champagne and… Sebastian.

Oh, boy. The champagne would have to wait for months, but Sebastian wouldn't.

The hours dragged by, and finally it was time to dress. Gracie chose a slinky scarlet gown, the high-low hemline making a statement of its own. She wore tall heels and her best gold jewelry, along with wide hoop earrings. Glancing in the mirror, she could see her baby bump was evident now, the slightest little rounding of her belly filling her heart with immeasurable pride.

When Sebastian pulled up to her home, she was ready and greeted him at the door.

"Wow," he said immediately. "You look gorgeous."

"Thank you. So do you. Handsome, I mean. Do you want to come in?"

He took her hand. "Trust me, you don't want me to come in. If I did…"

She couldn't argue with his logic. He was right. She'd never get over seeing him look so dashing in a dark suit and tie, his facial hair groomed just enough to make him look sexy and dangerous. She'd missed him, both in and out of bed.

He kissed her cheek again and helped her on with her coat. With a hand to her back, he walked her to his car and opened the door. "Where are we going?" she asked as she slipped into the passenger seat. His gaze roamed over her legs, and a swell of heat shot through her body.

"You'll see."

He was being cryptic all of a sudden, and she didn't know what to think.

"It's someplace special to me. To us."

He started the engine and turned on the music. The song playing was from her favorite band. Softly, she sang along with the tune, her voice no match for theirs, and yet it put a smile on Sebastian's face. Had he remembered her favorite music?

They headed down the road, away from her house, and after ten minutes, he pulled up to the Texas Cattleman's Club. Her brows rose in surprise. What was he up to?

The question in her eyes prompted him to say, "This will all make sense soon."

He helped her out of the car, and hand in hand, they

entered the club. After they checked in, the receptionist said, "Everything's ready for you, Mr. Wingate."

"Thank you."

She handed him a key and Sebastian led them down
a hallway to a private room. He stopped to open the
door and ushered her inside. The room was magical,
with dozens of lit candles, a roaring, wood-burning fire
in the fireplace and arrangements of beautiful flowers
throughout the room. In the middle of all of it, a table
was set for two.

She turned to face Sebastian, her face probably revealing her awe. "This is amazing. You did all this
today?"

He nodded. "I had to work fast. It was worth it to
see the look on your face. But before we talk about the
future, I need to talk to you about the past."

Sebastian pulled out a chair for her, and she took a
seat. Then, sitting down to face her, he took her hand.
It was as if he needed the connection, needed to touch
her in order to proceed. "It isn't easy for me to admit
this, but I've made a lot of mistakes with you. And I
hope to rectify all of them tonight, Gracie. First of all,
thank you for hearing me out. I want us to start out with
a fresh slate, so I'll admit to not being perfect."

"Nobody is," she said. In her youth, she'd thought
of him that way. Her crush had known no bounds. But
she was steeped in reality now. "I'm not perfect, either."

"From where I'm sitting at the moment, I'd say you
are." He scanned over her face, gazing into her eyes.

She smiled, loving the way his hand was softly squeezing hers, as if he needed her strength to go on.

"I was never after your money. Never. The thought never once crossed my mind. The Wingates are financially sound, and whatever struggles we have will be taken care of professionally. You bought the house, and that helped us, yes, but it was never about money between you and me. In fact, I wasn't thrilled that you thought so little of me."

"I didn't want to, Sebastian, but there were so many other things that confused me, too."

He inhaled. "I know, sweetheart. And that's on me. I wasn't sure about how to convince you about my feelings for you. You seemed to have the notion that I only cared about the baby, that I never wanted you because you weren't good enough for a Wingate. That I never seemed interested in you before this." He released a ragged breath. "But the truth is, I had a thing for you, too, Gracie. I just never acted on it because your father worked for us. And also because you were Beth's best friend. In my mind, you were off-limits. So yes, I never thought of us as a possible couple, but not because I didn't think you were worthy. And certainly not because I felt superior to you.

"More recently, I thought it best not to bombard you with my growing feelings because I didn't want to rush you. You seemed to need time, and I thought I was doing what you wanted. So I held back. Perhaps I shouldn't have. But I've always cared for you, Gracie. Make no mistake about that."

He squeezed her hand. "You may not even realize it, but you turn heads when you walk into a room. And to know that you're carrying my baby only makes you more beautiful to me."

Tears welled in her eyes. This time, she wouldn't blame it on hormones. This time, it was hearing Sebastian open up his heart that gave her hope and brought on deep emotion.

"About Rhonda," he began.

She held her tongue, keeping her promise to his ex that she wouldn't divulge anything they'd spoken about. Besides, it was better to hear it from him.

"I was only trying to help Rhonda's younger brother..."

Gracie listened to his full explanation and to his apology. She already had forgiven him in her heart. "I understand. It was a good thing you were trying to do."

"I'm still trying. I plan to be in the boy's life to a degree."

"I wouldn't expect anything less, but why didn't you just tell me about it? Didn't you trust me?"

"I—I didn't want to rock the boat. It was hard earning your trust, Gracie, and I wasn't sure I had it at the time. I gave my word to keep Lonny's problems private. It wouldn't have done anyone any good to bring light to his troubles."

She nodded. "I get that, Sebastian. I really do. You were trying to protect Lonny, just like I was trying to protect our baby. I, uh, I probably shouldn't have jumped to conclusions about you. I thought the worst of you, when in my heart, I'd always believed you were a good guy. I guess that's why I was so confused and hurt."

He squeezed her hand once again, keeping their connection solid. "I made a mess of things, but you have to know, I didn't want to fail our baby the way I failed Lonny in the past."

"I understand that." But she had to ask. She had to clear the air, and even though it was hard for her to do, she couldn't let this go without an explanation. "I guess what hurt me the most was when I proposed to you, and you looked like the devil had cornered you in the bowels of hell."

Sebastian began shaking his head. "Oh, man, Gracie. No, that's not how I felt at all. You just startled me, because I'd made so many mistakes with you, I wanted to be the one to do the proposing. I wanted to sweep you off your feet the way you deserve. I wanted to show you how much you meant to me. I had this all planned out in my head, and so—"

"I jumped the gun."

"I was thrilled you wanted to get married, but you deserve a beautiful wedding proposal. Can you understand that?"

Candles flickered, the fireplace shot blue and golden embers up, and Sebastian's love surrounded her. "I can. I do."

"Hold that thought, Gracie. Just hold that thought."

Sebastian rose from his chair and walked to her side. Then he bent his knee and brought out a gorgeous red velvet ring box. Her heart began to pound, and her body trembled as she gazed down at Sebastian, love shining in his eyes. He lifted the box lid to reveal a stunning oval diamond ring surrounded by dozens of tiny diamonds. It was the prettiest ring Gracie had ever seen.

"Gracie, we started out right here in these rooms when I met a wonderful masked woman who knocked me for a loop. I'd never felt that way before, the instant connection we had, the way we responded to each other. It wasn't a fluke that we're together now. We were meant to be, Gracie. I believe that with my whole heart. I love you so much. I love the baby you're carrying, too, and I want this love to continue on until we take our last breaths. Gracie Diaz, my love, will you be my wife? Will you marry me?"

Tears streamed down Gracie's face. She'd wanted this since childhood, and now she believed in Sebastian and his love. She believed they belonged together. She believed in the beautiful family they'd created. "I love you, too, Sebastian. I want nothing more than to be your wife. Yes, I'll marry you. Yes. Yes. *Yes!*"

He took her hand and placed the diamond ring on her finger. Then he pulled her up from the seat and cradled her face in his hands. "I love you, Gracie." And the kiss he bestowed upon her spoke of love and promise and forever. She'd never been happier.

"There's more, sweetheart," he said. He pulled a few papers out of his pocket. "This is the deed to your house. It's in your name now, and all yours. And here's an agreement proving I was never after your money.

It says we each keep what we went into our marriage with, so there'll never be any doubt."

"There never will be, Sebastian. Because I'm never letting you go."

He gave her another tantalizing kiss, and then took her by the hand. "Remember that little alcove, when we first—"

"Hooked up?"

"Made love," he corrected and then nuzzled her neck, his mouth working magic on her.

She ached for him. It'd been too long. "Think we can find it again?"

"I'm sure of it, sweetheart." He pointed to the far end of the room and the hidden space between the fireplace and a large bookshelf. "Right there."

She opened her mouth in awe, surprise and delight, then threw her arms around his neck and kissed him for all he was worth.

He took her hand and led her to the alcove. "This is where it all began…"

"If you wanted to sweep me off my feet, you've succeeded. Sebastian Wingate, you just might be perfect after all."

He touched her belly lovingly and his warmth brought joy to her heart. "That makes three of us, my love."

# Epilogue

*One year later...*

Gracie stood beside the podium, her husband at the helm, his voice deep and proud as he addressed the gathered crowd in the main dining hall of the Texas Cattleman's Club. "Let me start out by saying my wife, Gracie Diaz Wingate, has accomplished so much in her life, and no one deserves this honor more than she does. She's a dynamo, and frankly, this Wingate has trouble keeping pace with her. As you all know, she's incredibly smart. Well, she married me, didn't she?"

The small crowd, including his mother, Ava, and Lauren, Sutton, Beth and Cam, all chuckled at his little joke. The others in their family were off on their own adventures and couldn't be there today.

"She's also a wonderful mother to our beautiful infant son, Mateo." Sebastian choked up and Gracie was one compliment away from tears spilling down her cheeks, as well. She had only to look down at the precious baby in her arms to realize how very fortunate she was. She had a loving husband, a baby she adored and a place in the Royal community now.

"But all personal feelings aside, Gracie Diaz Wingate is a capable businesswoman, restaurateur and horse breeder. She loves each enterprise equally, and has recently opened a new office in the downtown area, where she plans on starting up an events business. I know she's thrilled to be the newest inductee to the Texas Cattleman's Club. So, with that said, I invite my beautiful wife to say a few words before we let the president do the honors."

Gracie handed the baby over to Sebastian, the transfer seamless. They'd been sharing baby duties ever since the little one took his first breath, and loving every second of it. Gracie's mother and brother had been here for the birth and had helped out for weeks while she and Sebastian got the hang of parenting and schedules and sleepless nights.

She stood in front of the podium now, looking into the eyes of her new family and so many other community members and friends. "I stand here before you, humbled and grateful for all the good things in my life. So many of my dreams have come true, two of them standing right beside me." Gracie looked upon Sebastian and Mateo lovingly and then turned back to the small crowd. "But to be here among all of you as part of this club, as part of the Royal community, is an honor I hope to live up to. I hope to make a difference in our town. And I plan to play a very active role at TCC. Thank you all for being here today. It means a great deal to me."

Then the president came up to say a few words. After his speech, Sebastian invited everyone in attendance to enjoy their dinner and music afterward. It had been his idea to celebrate Gracie's induction with a party for family and friends. Gracie loved him now more than ever. He'd proven himself to be the man she'd always hoped he was. The man she'd fantasized and loved for many years.

And now with Wingate Enterprises back on solid ground, Sebastian had only good things to look forward to. She sat beside him at a table, while dinner was being served. Piped-in music flowed throughout the room, and pastries would be served later. She got the feeling Beth had something to do with planning this party in her honor. As a sigh escaped her lips, Sebastian peered at her.

"What is it, sweetheart? Everything okay?"

She nodded and gazed at the two men in her life. "Yes, I'm great." She whispered quietly, "Just a little tired. I can't wait to go home with the two of you."

She lived on the beautiful sprawling land of the Wingate Estate now, in the home she'd decorated with the slightest of touches to make it their own.

"Of course," he whispered back. "It's been a long day."

"I love being with you and Mateo at our home. Maybe he will even sleep tonight."

"If not, it's my turn to rock him. Even though I think he prefers his mommy's arms. Can't say I blame him. I kinda like them, too." Sebastian kissed the side of her neck, his warm breath making every cell in her body come alive. Her husband was such a deliberate temptation, and she loved that about him.

She knew in her heart that the day she and Sebastian fell in love was the day of her true lottery win.

She couldn't get much luckier than that.

\* \* \* \* \*

*Don't miss the start of the next series set in Royal—Texas Cattleman's Club: Heir Apparent*

Back in the Texan's Bed *by Naima Simone Available February 2021!*

*When Charlotte Jarrett returns to Royal, Texas, with a child, no one's more surprised than her ex-lover, oil heir Ross Edmond. Determined to claim his son, he entices her to move in with him. But can rekindled passion withstand the obstacles tearing them apart?*

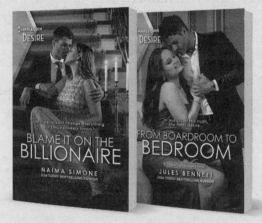

SPECIAL EXCERPT FROM

### ⓗ HARLEQUIN

# DESIRE

*Shy housekeeper Monica Darby has always had feelings for handsome chef and heir to his family's fortune Gabe Cress. But one unexpected night of passion and a surprise inheritance changes everything. With meddling families and painful pasts, will they find their happily-ever-after?*

*Read on for a sneak peek at*
One Night with Cinderella
*by nationally bestselling author Niobia Bryant!*

"Hopefully everyone will get home safe," she said.

Gabe took in her high cheekbones, the soft roundness of her jaw and the tilt of her chin. The scent of something subtle but sweet surrounded her. He forced his eyes away from her and cleared his throat. "Hopefully," he agreed as he poured a small amount of champagne into his flute.

"I'll leave you to celebrate," Monica said.

With a polite nod, Gabe took a sip of his drink and set the bottle at his feet, trying to ignore the reasons why he was so aware of her. Her scent. Her beauty. Even the gentle night winds shifting her hair back from her face. Distance was best. Over the past week he had fought to do just that to help his sudden awareness of her ebb. Ever since the veil to their desire had been removed, it had been hard to ignore.

She turned to leave, but moments later a yelp escaped her as her feet got twisted in the long length of her robe and sent her body careening toward him as she tripped.

Reacting swiftly, he reached to wrap his arm around her waist and brace her body up against his to prevent her fall. He let the hand holding his flute drop to his side. Their faces were just precious